Cleaning Up the Mess: Stories

by
Paul F. Ferguson

CLEANING UP THE MESS: STORIES. Copyright © 2000 by Paul F. Ferguson. All rights reserved. No part of this book may be reproduced or transmitted in any form or by any means, electronic or mechanical, including photocopying, scanning, recording, or by any information storage and retrieval system, without written permission from the Publisher except in the case of brief quotations embodied in critical reviews and articles.

Published in the United States of America by:

Scrivenery Press
P.O. Box 740969-1003
Houston, TX 77274-0969
http://www.scrivenery.com

First Edition

This is a work of fiction. Names, characters, places, and incidents, unless otherwise specifically noted, either are the product of the author's imagination or are used fictitiously.

"Cleaning Up the Mess" and "The Beast" were originally published in *Santa Barbara Review*, 1997 and 1999, respectively. The four-line poem at the beginning of "He Wasn't There Again Today" is from "Antigonish" by William Hughes Mearns, 1899. "The Temptations of Guthlac" is based on Paul F. Ferguson's original translation of an Old English poem from the *Exeter Book* edited by George Philip Krapp and Elliott Van Kirk Dobbie, Columbia University Press, 1936. "The Glass Tree" is based on an Irish folk tale transcribed by Jeremiah Curtin in *Myths and Folk-Lore of Ireland*, Little, Brown, and Company, 1889.

Cover design by Françoise Merot, based upon a photograph by Kaz Chiba. Editing by Leila Joiner. The book block is digitally typeset in Minion *and* Minion Expert, *by Adobe Systems Incorporated (www.adobe.com).*

00   01   02   03   SP   10   9   8   7   6   5   4   3   2   1

LIBRARY OF CONGRESS CATALOG CARD NUMBER **00-112026**

ISBN **1-893818-08-X**

This collection is dedicated, with much love, to my wife, Cam, whose life I have complicated for thirty years.

Contents

The Glass Tree: A Tale of Ancient Ireland 1
First Kill 29
Consecration 41
911 55
Cleaning Up the Mess 69
House in the Country 83
The Temptations of Guthlac 99
The Art of Courtly Loving 113
First Step 129
The Beast 141
The Spirit of Things 145
He Wasn't There Again Today 165

The Glass Tree: A Tale of Ancient Ireland

"The son of the King of Ireland," the old man intones, seated in his chair like a king himself, the smoke from his pipe swirling around his head like mist from the mountains, "was a handsome lad whose hair was as black as the darkest night, and whose eyes were as blue as the sea.

"On his eighteenth birthday, the King and Queen of Ireland gave him a golden harp and a golden horn, which he learned to play more beautifully than anyone else in the kingdom. Even the court musicians, who were famous throughout the land, envied the boy's ability."

The grandson finds himself mildly interested. He expected his grandfather to start on something like "The Frog Prince" or "Three Billy Goats Gruff" or another of those tales he has told a million times. The boy continues to shuffle the deck of cards in his hand, but glances up at the old man, who sucks softly on his pipe.

"One day, the son of the King of Ireland wandered about the countryside, playing his golden harp and singing to himself. The sun stood high in the sky, and he sat under a tree to rest. He had not been there long when he heard a whistle behind him, and turned to see a giant hurrying in his direction. The giant's teeth were long and yellow; his nose was large and crooked. Black, greasy hair dripped down from his head like spilled gravy. The son of the King of Ireland felt the heart in his chest pounding.

"The giant stood with his hands on his hips before the boy.

"'That certainly is a fine harp you have there,' he said.

"'Yes it is,' said the son of the King of Ireland. 'The finest harp in the kingdom.'

"'I would like to own a harp like that.'

"'It's not for sale,' said the boy.

"'Well,' said the giant, running the back of his hand along his jaw line, 'I would do almost anything to own that harp. I could kill you, you know, and take it from you.'

"'You could do that,' said the boy. 'But my father would send his soldiers out to kill you and bring the harp back, and you would be worse off than you were before.'

"'True enough,' said the giant. 'But I wouldn't kill you anyway, and not because I fear your father and his soldiers. I would like to own that harp, but not by stealing it. Do you by any chance play cards?'

"'I do, indeed,' said the son of the King of Ireland.

"'Perfect. To make things fair, we will wager your harp against all my land so that you don't go away empty-handed if you win.'

"The giant pulled a pack of cards from beneath his jerkin and began to shuffle. The pack was old, dog-eared, and smudged from being handled so much. When the giant finished shuffling, he dealt six cards, one at a time, to himself and to the son of the King of Ireland. The boy led the six of hearts, but the giant trumped it and took the first hand. But when the giant led back, the son of the King of Ireland trumped him with the ace and took the remaining cards to win the giant's land.

"'You are quite a card player and have won my estate fairly. But tomorrow we shall play again.'

"The giant spread his mouth wide in a grin that exposed all his teeth as if to remind the youth how fragile he was, then lumbered off into the distance."

The pipe has gone out. The old man examines the bowl, decides there is still tobacco in it, and lights the pipe again. He draws in several times and finally blows out a puff of smoke that billows around him like a storm cloud. The boy watches his grandfather, waiting for him to resume the story, impatient for the old man to get on with it. He glances at the clock on the mantle, then turns over one of the cards he has been shuffling.

It is the six of hearts.

The following day, the king's son went to the same place, this time carrying the golden horn. He didn't have long to wait. Hardly had he seated himself beneath a tree to shade himself from the glare of the sun when the ground began to shake and he saw the giant climbing up the hill, knocking aside trees as if they were spindles.

"And what have you brought for me today?"

"I have brought this golden horn." The king's son held up the horn, which sparkled so brightly in the sunlight that the giant had to hold his hands up in front of his face and peer through his fingers so he wouldn't be blinded by it.

"It certainly looks good," said the giant. "But does it sound as good as it looks?"

The boy raised the horn to his lips and began to play a melody so sweet and clear that even the giant didn't look quite as ugly as before.

"That would certainly be a lovely thing to own," said the giant. "I don't suppose you'd think of selling it."

"Of course not."

"And I've already agreed not to kill you and steal it from you. So here is my wager. I have five hundred bulls with silver hooves. You can see them grazing in the meadowlands below us. I shall wager them against your golden horn."

Again the giant took a deck of cards from his leather jerkin, dealt them, and gestured for the king's son to lead the first card.

And again the giant lost.

"Pah!" said the giant. "You are a very fortunate card player, my young friend. But your luck cannot hold out forever. Let us play one more time, tomorrow."

"Agreed," said the king's son.

The giant stood and grinned down at him, again exposing his jagged teeth, which looked just a bit sharper and more dangerous than they had the day before. But the youth bowed to the giant and led home the five hundred bulls with the silver hooves.

When the bulls were driven in and he had received great praise from all the court for his cleverness, the son of the King of Ireland sought the blind court sage who had frequently chided him for being too clever.

"Have I not proved myself grandly?" he said to the old man.

The old man smacked his lips and tapped his staff upon the stone floor. "That 'e have," he said. "But mind me, Ireland's son. Don't go the giant's way a third time, for if 'e play with 'im again, 'e will rue it."

The young man laughed.

"Don't worry yourself, old father. The giant plays foolishly. He throws away his trumps, overbids his hands. And I believe his eyesight is bad, for he cannot tell his king from his jack."

The blind sage shook his head, his mouth drawn down in sadness. "Mind me. 'e will rue it if 'e go out again."

But nothing could keep the King of Ireland's son from playing a third time. Despite the sage's advice, when the third day came, away he went and sat beneath the same tree on the same hillside.

A long time he waited, but no one came. The sky grew dark, black clouds gathered overhead, and the young man began to fear he would be caught in the storm. Just as he was about to leave, he heard a whistle and saw the giant thundering toward him.

"Well, son of the King of Ireland." He planted himself before the youth like the oldest of oak trees, then leaned forward until his face blocked out the sky. "What shall we play for today?"

"I have brought nothing with me save only myself," said the youth.

"Indeed," said the giant. "And you expect me to wage nothing against nothing? Where is the pleasure in that?"

"Not at all," said the boy. "For you have brought with you something of value."

"And what is that, pray tell?"

"You have your head, and I have mine. We shall play for each other's heads, and the third time shall pay for all."

Lightning flashed behind the giant, thunder rolled, bounding across the hills and back like boulders rolling down a mountain. A gruesome smile lit up the giant's face and he drew the cards from his jerkin. "Just so," he said, and winked once at the boy. "The third time shall pay for all."

The son of the King of Ireland stiffened. He did not like the way the giant's eyes shone, or the way the spittle drooled from his lips and puddled on the ground, but since it was too late to call back his words, he picked up the cards the giant had dealt him.

Trick after trick fell to the giant, and when the last trick fell, an ace placed upon the boy's queen, the young man had lost the game. The boy's stomach began to quiver; his head felt light. The giant sat back and laughed a great laugh that rumbled through the hills and shook the high heavens so that rain began to fall.

"Hear me, son of the King of Ireland. I have won the game and your head. But I will show mercy and give you time to settle your affairs. In a year and a day, you will come to my castle to pay what you owe. There is no help for it. Should you fail to pay your debt, I will ravage your father's kingdom and slay everyone in it. Remember our wager."

With that, the giant lumbered off over the hill and was gone.

For a long time the young man sat on the high hillside staring at the space where the giant had finished, praying that what had happened had been something he'd dreamed. But when drops of rain the size of gold coins spattered against his skin, and the giant's footprints filled with water, turning them into standing pools, he knew there would be no awakening, that he must lose his head.

He returned home sad and weary. When the king and queen saw him, they knew that a great burden was on him. His face was pale; a distant look was in his eyes. He did not, could not speak to them, but went straight inside and refused to eat or drink. That night, and for many nights after, he wept bitterly for the trouble he had brought upon himself.

The old man pauses to ream the ashes from his pipe. His face is somber, but as he raises his eyes, the grandson sees something in them sparkle. The boy glances down at the playing cards in his hands, then back at his grandfather. The old man does not look at him at all, but devotes his attention to cleaning and refilling his pipe as if the boy were not even there.

"Is that all?" the boy asks.

"Nope," answers the old man. "There's more."

"Well?" says the boy.

"In good time."

The grandfather lights the pipe slowly, savoring its flavor. Then, settling himself more comfortably in the chair and sucking on his dentures by way of prologue, he continues.

The seasons passed, spring into summer, summer to autumn. Winter's raging winds wrestled the sun and kept her captive until the very ground was locked in ice. Soon the soothing rains of spring awakened the tiny buds, but no such rains could soothe the fearful heart of the son of the King of Ireland.

Finally, the time came for him to seek the giant's castle and deliver himself up. On the eve of his departure, the blind sage tapped his way along the corridors to the boy's chamber and stood before the youth like a withered thorn bush.

"'e have been a proper fool, Ireland's son."

"I know, old father."

"'e have been so clever 'e have outsmarted 'eerself."

"You speak true, old father, and I blame none other than myself."

"That is well. What is past cannot be undone. I come to speak of what lies ahead. I know this giant 'e seek. 'e has a great castle, and around the walls of the castle are iron spikes, and on the spikes are the heads of foolish boys who played cards with the giant and lost. There is one spike empty, but it is for 'e it waits unless 'e practice wisdom.

"As 'e follow the road, 'e will come to a fork. Take the right fork and follow it 'til midday. There 'e shall come to a lake whose surface is silver. Rest at that lake, drink of its waters, and do what 'e are called to do."

The boy stared at the old man, puzzled.

"And what would that be?" he asked.

"How should I know," said the sage. "I cannot tell the future. All I can tell 'e is that the lake of silver is the beginning of wisdom."

The old man shuffled out of the boy's chamber and left him alone in the gathering darkness.

That night the boy's dreams were troubled by visions of severed heads and a lake gleaming silver in the moonlight. At dawn, without a word to the king and queen, he departed, heading north. Soon he came to a fork and took the right path as the sage had bid. When the sun reached its zenith, the young man stood before a lake with a silver surface. He reached down and scooped up the sweetest handful of water he had ever tasted. Then he heard a trill of laughter. Swimming in the lake was the most beautiful maiden he had ever seen. Her hair was as bright as the brightest gold, her skin as fair as the whitest ivory. In an instant he felt he must be in love with her. His heart thumped inside his chest as he watched her, thoroughly enchanted by her beauty. He found himself paralyzed as she swam toward him.

When she emerged from the lake, she seemed not at all concerned with her nakedness, but faced him as resolutely as if she were fully dressed. Beads of water sparkled like jewels against her fair breast.

"Who are you?" she asked.

The son of the King of Ireland started to speak his name, but thought better of it. Despite her beauty, she could easily be a witch, an enchantress. The court magicians had often said that the forests were filled with witches. And giving one's name was to give a witch power over you.

"That I will not tell you," he said.

"What have you done with my clothes?"

"Clothes?" he said. Of course, she must have clothes somewhere around here. He turned his head and saw them draped on a branch behind him. Quickly, he dashed to the branch and took them down.

"Give them to me," she said.

"First, you must grant me a favor."

She folded her arms across her breasts and looked straight into his eyes.

"I grant no favors, especially under duress. Give me my clothes at once."

"Not until I have your word."

"Suit yourself," she said, and turned to leave.

The young man's heart sank as she walked unconcerned toward a grove. Surely the sage could not have been mistaken. He had made it sound so easy. The youth was supposed to find wisdom at the lake. How could she just walk away from him, naked? How could she know he wouldn't attack her? But attacking her really wouldn't help him, would it? The thought of his own severed head impelled the son of the King of Ireland to follow her. She had to help him.

"Wait," he cried. "I must have your help."

She turned and fixed him with her eye.

"My clothes."

"But..."

"It is discourteous and unbecoming to steal a lady's gown. I make no promises to such a man."

Again the maiden folded her arms and looked at him with eyes that penetrated his soul. The son of the King of Ireland felt as if it were he who was naked, that the maiden could read every thought inside his head, know every secret he ever had, know every ignoble thing he had ever done, and his face grew warm.

"Very well," he said, and handed the maiden her gown.

When the maiden was dressed, she addressed the young man.

"I know where you are going, and I know about your bargain. I don't know why I'm bothering to help you. You are more trouble than you are worth. If he offers you meat or drink, don't take it. Whatever he asks, do it. Then wait until I come. If you follow my instructions, you may yet save your life."

The son of the King of Ireland nodded his head dumbly. At that moment, he would have done anything she asked. She was so beautiful to look at, he felt something leap in his chest and thought he must be in love with her, even though her voice was cold and businesslike and her eyes flashed silver. She mounted a coal black horse trimmed with silver tackle and rode off.

The youth trotted after her, but the horse was obviously too fast for him, and he lost sight of her before much longer. Shortly before twilight, he came to a broad field and stopped short. Before him lay the castle of the giant. He had never seen anything quite so large. The walls stretched to the left and right for what seemed like miles and rose before him like a cliff. And just as the sage had said, atop the wall ran countless spikes of black iron, each holding the head of a young man. One spike was empty. The youth touched his throat without thinking and gulped once.

Screwing up his courage, he announced his arrival to the stone walls, and the massive wooden gate swung open.

The giant stood in the center of the courtyard studying the young man, hands upon his hips, a grin spreading across his face. His black hair was neatly brushed, and he wore a flowing crimson robe with gold piping.

"Welcome, my friend. You keep your word well."

He led the young man across the courtyard toward a large table that was laden with all sorts of meat, fruit, and bread.

"Come," said the giant. "Share with me some meat from my stable and some mead from my barrels."

The young man was about to sit down and gorge himself, he was so hungry. His stomach gurgled at the thought of that sumptuous roast at the table's center, and those wondrous fruit pies with the succulent golden crusts, but the youth recalled the maiden's words, closed his eyes and tried to gather his resolve.

"I thank you for your kindness," he said. "But I prefer neither food nor drink. My journey has been long and tiring and I am in need of rest."

"Very well. I've never heard a young man refuse a free meal before. But that's your choice," said the giant. "Come. I will show you your bed."

The giant led the young man to a deep cistern, pushed him in, and locked the door behind him.

"Hey," yelled the son of the King of Ireland. "Wha..." He'd started to say, "What is going on?" but the waters closed over his head and he found himself sinking. He kicked his legs to struggle to the surface. For several minutes, he fought to keep himself afloat, but the waters turned his limbs numb and he felt as if something were trying to tug him under.

The young man was in despair. "Whatever he asks, do it," she had said, and now he was drowning, never to see his home again. He should have known better than to trust her. She was probably colluding with her father to build up his confidence, trick him into believing she was on his side, then toss him into a cistern to drown.

Just as his limbs started to tremble from the chill and he was about to give in to the force that pulled him down, the cistern door opened and the maiden with the golden hair and silver eyes seized him by the wrist and pulled him out.

"About time," he wheezed.

"Quiet," she said. "You have no faith."

She told him to strip. When his clothes lay in a sodden mess at his feet, she wrapped him in a woolen blanket and led him to her chamber, fed him on fruit, cheese, and bread, and gave him a soft bed on which to rest.

"Don't ask," she said, then put out the candle and withdrew from the chamber, leaving him alone in the darkness. He closed his eyes and tried to call up her image, but before he could do so, he was asleep.

Shortly before daybreak, she woke him and handed him his clothes. They had dried overnight.

"Put these on," she said. "And hurry."

"Where are we going?"

She didn't answer, but grabbed his hand and led him back to the cistern.

"Now wait a minute," he protested.

"Sh," she said. "There's no time. He'll be here in a few minutes. Just do what he tells you." Then she pushed him into the water and closed the door behind her.

The son of the King of Ireland was still spluttering when the giant opened the door and yelled, "Have you rested well, my young friend?"

"That I glub," said the young man, and started to choke on the water that had found its way down his throat.

The giant reached down and lifted the son of the King of Ireland from the cistern by the scruff of his neck and set him at a wooden table.

"You look well rested," he said. "And it's well that you are, for there is much you need to do today. Do you see that stable over there?"

He pointed across the courtyard and the youth looked in the direction the giant's finger was pointing. His jaw dropped open in dismay. What the giant called a stable was the size of a small city as far as the young man was concerned.

"I have this problem," the giant continued. "It seems that my great-grandmother—God rest her soul—lost a lovely silver comb in there when she was a girl. That was a long time ago, a hundred years, as a matter of fact. She was never able to find it. Neither was I. But here's the bargain I offer. If you can manage to clean that stable out and find that comb by sunset, I just might let you keep your head. How does that strike you?"

Wonderful, thought the boy. The comb has been missing for four generations and the giant expected him to find it by sundown. What a sick sense of humor he had. The boy might as well kiss his head goodbye now and be done with it.

"And to help you out, I've brought you these." The giant took out two shovels, an old one and a new one. The old one was covered with rust, the end eaten off by years of digging into manure, the handle rough and covered with splinters. One good whack, and the whole thing would fall apart. The new one was bright and shiny, the blade so dark and smooth he was sure it had recently come from the smithy's forge.

"Choose," said the giant. The son of the King of Ireland took the new one (why would he even consider the old one?) and went to work.

The inside of the stable was worse than he had expected. The odor of horse piss nearly gagged him and he had to wrap a rag around his nose to cut the smell. Even so, his eyes still watered, and he had to stop every few minutes to wipe away the tears. Manure was piled high, nearly to the tops of the windows, and it amazed him that there was any room for horses. In fact, he didn't see any horses, and concluded that they only came here to empty their bowels and probably spent the rest of their time somewhere else.

Two hours he labored without taking a rest. His muscles ached, and torrents of sweat streamed down his chest, but for every shovelful he cleared, two more took its place. It was useless. The stable would never be clean. He sat among the mounds of manure and decaying straw and held his head in his hands, the head that would soon find itself skewered on a spike in front of the giant's castle.

While he was contemplating the meaninglessness of his own fate, the stable door opened and in came the giant's daughter. She was more radiant than he had remembered. Maybe she simply looked more beautiful because everything in the stable looked so awful. Her golden hair tumbled over her shoulders like water down a mountain stream, and her silver eyes shone.

"How are you thriving?" she asked. Her voice was cheery, as if everything were perfectly delightful.

"I am not thriving at all," said the king's son. "And how can you be so cheery when I'm going to lose my head."

"You worry too much," she said. "I'll help you."

And taking the old shovel, the one that was covered with rust and looked as if it would disintegrate if you even touched it, she began to clear the stable. Shovelful after shovelful of manure vanished as if it had never been, and when she was finished, she said, "Great-ma's silver comb is in the corner."

Sure enough, there in the corner was the silver comb, its back etched with runes. But when he turned to ask the giant's daughter how she had done that, she was gone.

At sundown, he strode up to the door of the giant's house and handed him the comb.

"Aha," said the giant, stroking his chin. "Cleverly done. Clever indeed. But you must be hungry."

Hungry? The boy was famished. His stomach began to growl and gurgle again. The boy's head filled with images of roasts, pies, tarts. But once again, the maiden's warning stopped him. "Take no meat or drink."

"No thanks," he said, and his stomach burbled in protest. The giant smirked. "It's been a long day and I simply need to rest," said the boy.

"Then rest you shall have," said the giant, and led the youth to the cistern and threw him in.

This time, the boy didn't even try to struggle. He put his head back, extended his arms to his side and let them flap loosely, and hoped he could hold on long enough for the maiden to get to him, assuming, of course, that she would come to his aid a second time.

Soon the giant was snoring (it sounded like thunder) and the golden-haired maiden again led him from the cistern to her chamber. She took his wet clothes, gave him a dry blanket, fed him, showed him to bed, then disappeared. He wished that she would stay and talk, just for a few minutes. He wanted to ask her why she was helping him. Did she hope that by doing him all these favors he would take her away from her cruel father? On the other hand, she didn't seem to dislike the giant, or even have much fear of him. But the maiden wouldn't linger. She told the young man to "shush" and closed the door.

In the morning, she returned him to the cistern.

"Are you awake in there?" called the giant.

"I am," said the young man.

"Well, then, come out. Nice job you did on that stable. I was impressed. But now that it's clean, I realized how shabby it looks. So I thought, you being such an expert on stables, that you might like to thatch its roof. Before sundown, of course."

"I suppose so," said the youth, and groaned to himself.

"I thought you'd agree," said the giant. "But there is a catch. You must thatch it with birds' feathers, no two feathers of the same color or of the same size, or guess what."

"My head will be forfeit," said the youth.

"Clever lad," said the giant.

The giant held out two whistles, an old one and a new one, the old one dented and cracked, the new one bright and shiny. It took the youth a few minutes to figure out that the whistles were for summoning birds, and he started to reach for the old whistle, reasoning that if the old shovel had worked for cleaning out the stable, the old whistle just might work for summoning the birds, but at the last minute he changed his mind. He'd heard court musicians trying to play old whistles and had to cover his ears the noise was so awful. He chose the new whistle and set out over the hills and valleys, whistling all the while.

He was more than a decent musician. Everyone at court knew it, and he had been trained by the best. So as he wandered up and down the hills, playing the whistle, he knew the sounds coming from it were the sweetest anyone would ever hear. But however hard he whistled, however sweetly he played, no birds came. When the sun was high overhead, he returned to the stable, his lips aching from whistling, and sat down to weep.

In an instant, the giant's daughter was beside him.

"Not doing well again today, I see," she said.

"Not at all," he said.

She tossed her head as if he were hopeless. "I suppose I'll have to help you again."

She brought a basket from outside and spread before him a meal of bread, wine, cheeses, and fruit, and bade him eat. He reached over and tore off a chunk of bread, broke off a bit of cheese and began to eat. He was suddenly famished. When he looked up again, he saw that somehow—he didn't know how—the stable was completely thatched with feathers, no two of the same color or kind. The giant's daughter had vanished.

Magic. He'd been right all along. The giant's daughter was a witch and had been using her magic to help him. He wasn't sure why she was helping him, what her motivation was, but if it helped him keep his head, he saw no reason not to let her continue, and be grateful for her help.

At sunset, the giant approached the stable. He inspected the roof, ran his hands gently over the feathers, sniffed them, oohed and ahhed over the beauty of the thing. Then he turned to the youth and arched his eyebrow.

"Lovely work. Expert, one might say. Hard to believe that one young man could be so talented."

The young man felt himself blush.

"In fact," said the giant, "it is so lovely I'm inclined to believe that you might have had a little help. Is that it?"

The young man froze. Did the giant know? Had his daughter told him, or perhaps left some obvious clue? He still couldn't help at least entertaining the idea that the giant and his daughter were playing some game with him, toying with him. But he couldn't be sure. What would happen if he admitted he had help? Would she get in trouble? Would the giant grow angry and behead him here and now?

"Not at all," replied the young man, praying that this small lie would save his life. "It was my own wit and skill. And now if you don't mind, I could really use some rest."

The giant stroked his chin and regarded the boy. For a moment, the youth was certain the giant knew the truth and would simply sever the head from his body where he stood. But instead, he lifted his head and laughed.

"Rest. Of course, rest. All living creatures need rest after a hard day's toil."

And he took the youth to the cistern to spend the night as he had the other two.

The next morning, finding him still alive in the cistern, the giant said to him, "Come out. There is much work to be done."

The boy stood dripping before the giant. He was beginning to grow weary of being tossed in the cistern every night, dragged out, made to do some stupid task that made absolutely no sense to him, then tossed back in the cistern again. It was humiliating and tiresome. He wished the giant would get it over with and cut his head off or let him go. There would be no more gambling for him, no more card playing. He had learned his lesson.

"Below my castle," said the giant, "far beneath the earth, is a tree of glass five hundred feet high, without a single branch save at the top where there is a crow's nest. In the nest is a single egg. I must have that egg for my supper tonight or your head will be forfeit."

A crow's egg? For dinner? Why couldn't the giant be satisfied with hens' eggs like everyone else? Why did it have to be a crow's egg, and one from a nest at the top of a glass tree, for God's sake?

The giant went about his business and left the young man to fend for himself.

The grandfather pauses, his brows knitted into a frown. The pipe has gone out. He studies the backs of his hands as if, the boy thinks, he has lost the thread of his own tale, or has found himself suddenly at the center of some labyrinth from which there is no escape. The boy shifts his position to compensate for the tingling in his legs, while his grandfather slowly surveys the room as if seeking some enchanted object to help him out of his dilemma. In a few moments, he lowers his head, staring at an invisible point in the carpet, and begins to speak once again, his voice soft and meditative.

For a long time, the son of the King of Ireland sat in deep thought. What was the giant's game? The giant could easily have lopped off the young man's head and set it upon the spike without such an elaborate prologue. Had he toyed with other kings' sons as he now toyed with the son of the King of Ireland? And if so, to what purpose?

He was being tested. That much was plain. But what was the point? To see what foolishness he would endure to avoid his own death? And what of the giant's daughter? Surely, she must know what her father was plotting. After all, when the youth met her at the silver lake, she had known who he was and where he was going. If she had known that much, she must also have known what would happen once he arrived at the castle.

Here the mystery deepened, for the son of the King of Ireland could not decide whether she was enemy or ally, her father's accomplice in the contest or a secret rebel against his perversity. He wanted to believe in the unconfirmed promise of her beauty, the promise that he could avoid death, and in her willingness to help him. He wanted to trust her, but some reckless part of him wanted to confront them both and shout, "No more of this! Get on with it!"

But the thought of the giant's cold blade on his neck, the vision of his own head, face bloated, tongue protruding, mounted on the spike, gave him pause. Perhaps it would be best to play the game to its conclusion, to hope, against all reason, that death was, finally, avoidable.

The son of the King of Ireland rose from thought and sought the cavern beneath the giant's castle. It did not take long to find, though it was partially concealed by bramble. A lighted torch stood just inside the entrance.

"Convenient," the young man said to the air around him.

He made his way through the dark tunnel, carefully sidestepping pits and chasms that receded into blackness, some so deep no echo ever returned from them. Dreadful vapors of burning tar and rotten eggs arose from the chasm and surrounded him like a shroud. Cobwebs brushed his face and caught in his eyelids; spiders scurried through his hair. Bats flitted past his ears with cries of "cree, cree." Serpents and toads slithered past his ankles or leaped out of the way at the sight of the torch's flame.

At length he reached his destination.

Though the giant had told him of the tree's height, the youth was not prepared for the sight that greeted him. The trunk of clear glass must have measured eight feet in diameter and rose majestically until it vanished into the darkness above. Its surface caught the flame of his torch and reflected it back in a thousand shards of brightness that seemed to swarm around him. A spring of clear water rushed and gurgled beyond the tree.

He placed the torch in a wall sconce and approached the tree. He tried to shake it, but to no avail. The tree would not budge. Then he tried to climb it, but he slipped down, it was so slick. He tried again, and again slipped down.

When he was sure he had failed and sat at the tree's base, despairing of his head, the giant's daughter stood before him.

Her appearance chilled him. No longer was she the beautiful maiden of the silver lake. Her skin was pale as rock, with a slightly purplish hue, and dark purple shadows circled her eyes. Her lips were thin and wan, turned down in what almost seemed like a grimace of anguish. Her fingers were long and thin, and for an instant he was certain he could see the bleached bones beneath her flesh. He hair, once golden, was now a sickly yellow, tangled and knotted. She glided toward him as if she were the fell spirit of the place.

"How are you thriving?" she asked. Her voice seemed to come from one of those bottomless chasms.

"Not well," he said. "You don't look very good, either. What has he done to you?"

The maiden's eyes flashed at him. "He has done nothing to me."

"Sorry," he said. "I didn't mean to offend you."

"I am not offended," she said.

He didn't know what else to say, so he said nothing for a long while. He looked around, avoiding the maiden's eyes, her ravaged appearance. It was painful to look at her. He looked up at the tree again, then at his surroundings, but there was nothing in the cavern that he could use to help him.

"It's no use," he said. "You must help me or I shall lose my head."

"I've helped you twice already."

The iciness of her words made him shiver, and he saw before him his own bloodied head. He wanted to run, but there was nowhere to run. Beads of sweat crystallized on his upper lip and he forced himself to speak.

"Y-you promised. We have an agreement."

"There is no promise."

"But at the silver lake you promised you would help me."

"You threatened to take my clothes. I told you I didn't make promises under duress. There was no agreement, no promise. I owe you nothing."

"But why have you helped me up to now?"

"Because I choose to. And because you need help. But I see you are still helpless, maybe even hopeless. You have learned nothing."

"What am I supposed to learn? Tell me."

The maiden shook her head in dismay. "Watch carefully. Pay attention. If I tell you more, you will learn nothing. Besides, I'm not sure it's worth it to help someone who can't tell the simple truth."

"Truth? What are you talking about?"

"You denied to my father that it was I who helped you."

The son of the King of Ireland was in despair. So this was the game. There were secret rules he knew nothing of. There was no way to win under such circumstances, but he must at least try to defend himself.

"I was trying to protect you. I feared he would harm you if he knew of your help." His words were a lie, and the son of the King of Ireland hoped that the giant's daughter would not detect his deception. The giant's daughter stared at him for a long moment, her lips pursed, her silver eyes penetrating his soul like needles penetrating brocade, and he could not detect whether she believed him or not. At length she spoke.

"I will save your life one more time, but you must keep faith with me. A time will come when I will ask you to give me something. You must give me whatever it is I ask."

With scarcely a thought, he replied, "Done." His heart stopped pounding, and he felt invigorated with the prospect of getting through this with his head intact.

The giant's daughter did not hesitate. From the pocket of her gown she drew a silver knife and handed it to the young man. The blade was long and curved, its edge and point sharp, and for a moment the boy thought she was going to plunge it into his chest or slit his throat with it. It would be like the giant to play that sort of joke on him. But she held the knife out to him, handle first.

"With this knife," she began, "you must kill me and strip the flesh from my bones. Wrap my flesh in the white samite you find by the spring. Then use my bones to climb the tree. They will stick to the tree as if they had grown there. When you come down, place your foot on each bone and it will drop into your hand as you touch it. Leave none untouched or it will stay behind. When you come to earth again, arrange my bones together on the samite, place my flesh over them, and sprinkle it with water from the spring. I shall stand before you whole. Do exactly as I tell you."

The grandson is stunned at this turn of events, and he would have interrupted his grandfather to ask one of the many questions that swims through his mind, but it is plain that the old man is captivated by his own tale. He puffs madly on his pipe, waves his arms back and forth in the air, purses his lips in an effort to mimic the maiden's voice. His eyes have a strange fire in them, as if the old man is possessed by some power greater than himself, something speaking through him, but not separate from him. The boy holds his questions, fearing to break the spell that holds both him and his grandfather. The tree of glass seems to be sprouting right there in the living room.

"But I can't kill you," protested the son of the King of Ireland. "I have never killed anyone before. It is against the law of God."

The maiden leaned forward, put her hand on his shoulder, brought her face to within mere inches, and looked straight into his eyes. Her breath smelled of ashes, and her skin looked as brittle as parchment. She spoke slowly, almost in a whisper, but with great solemnity, as if all of existence depended upon her next words.

"Do not be afraid. If you do what I tell you, all will be well. To save your life you must climb the tree, and to climb the tree you must take my life. The choice is yours."

The son of the King of Ireland ran his thumb across the knife edge. The thought of killing the giant's daughter made him shudder, but hadn't she already done wonders? Couldn't she do it again? She had told him a few days ago that he had no faith, and she was right. Or at least she was right then. This could all be a trick—a rather grisly trick, he had to admit—to tell him something so preposterous he simply had to back out. Or what she said, no matter how impossible it seemed, might be true. If he didn't kill her, he would never climb the tree, get the crow's egg, and would definitely lose his head. If he did kill her, things might work out as she had said, though he doubted it, or she would simply die an awful death and the giant would kill him anyway. Though this was probably nothing more than another trick designed to add murder to his growing list of transgressions, he was also consumed by a fierce desire to believe that what she said was true.

With trembling hands, he raised the knife high above her and plunged it into the center of her chest. The maiden let out a cry of pain that echoed off the cavern walls and caused the glass tree to ring in response, then she slumped to the ground. Blood gushed from her breast, flooding over the young man's hands and spattering his shirt. He had never seen so much blood before. His head swam and he tumbled forward, but caught himself and shook off the queasiness. Very carefully, fighting off waves of nausea, he slit the maiden down the center of the breastbone to where her legs joined and peeled back the flesh.

The grandson's eyes widen and his mouth drops open. He feels lightheaded, but can not tear his eyes from his grandfather. The old man has discarded his pipe and slid from his armchair to the floor, where he now kneels, his hands drawing an invisible knife across the flesh of an invisible maiden with golden hair. The boy, convinced that his grandfather has gone mad, wants to call for help, for his grandmother, father, mother, but there is no one else in the house. All he can do is watch as the old man plays out this fantasy, this tale that started innocently enough, but seems now to have sucked him all the way into it like a sinkhole.

The son of the King of Ireland wrapped the daughter's flesh in the white samite, as she had instructed him, disjointed the bones, then turned to the tree. He attached the first bone to the glass trunk and was astonished to find that it held fast as she said it would. He attached the second, then the third, then began to climb, mounting one at a time, fastening the bones—shin bone, thigh bone, fibula, and tibia—and using them as steps until he came to the crow's nest and stood on the last bone, which happened to be the bleach-white skull of the maiden.

There was the egg. He reached for it, placed it in a pouch inside his jerkin. His head was saved. Though he could not know it with absolute certainty, he felt this would be the last of the trials—these things have a way of happening in threes—and the giant would let him return home to his father, mother, and kingdom. He felt like doing a jig, but the top of a maiden's skull five hundred feet above a rock floor with nothing to break his fall was not the best place for it, so he scrambled down the tree as quickly as he could, yanking each bone from its place as he made his descent. In his eagerness, he placed his foot on every bone but the last, which was so close to the ground he neglected it.

Then he reassembled the bones, one by one, and it took him quite a long time. There were so many bones he wasn't sure where they all went, but in the end, realizing his time was growing short, he jumbled them all together and hoped for the best. Then he draped the flesh over them and sprinkled it with water from the spring. In an instant the giant's daughter stood before him.

Her skin was still pale, and her eyes had turned from silver to grey slate. She looked at the son of the King of Ireland with dismay.

"It is finished," she said, then added more in sorrow than in anger, "but see what you've done," and gestured toward the tree. The neglected bone gleamed at the tree's base like a lost star.

It was then he noticed that the maiden's left leg was deformed, twisted under her. Without another word, she turned away from him and hobbled off into the darkness.

"Wait," he called after her. "It was a mistake. I didn't mean it."

But the maiden was gone and his own words echoed back to him. He wanted to smash the crow's egg, to tell the giant he was tired of these games and he didn't want to play any more. The glass tree glittered above him like the dome of the universe.

That night, when he handed the giant the crow's egg, the giant said, "You have had help."

The son of the King of Ireland hesitated, tempted at first to deny any help, but fearing the giant's wrath, responded, "It was your daughter who helped me."

The giant glared at him for a long moment, then laughed a great laugh that rumbled through the castles, shook the walls, made the windows tremble, and caused books to come tumbling from their shelves.

"So be it," said the giant. "If my daughter has helped you, she has reasons of her own. Go now. The debt is paid."

So the son of the King of Ireland returned home, never stopping until he came to the castle of his father. The king and queen embraced him and wept for joy to find their son was not dead.

The grandfather has resumed his place in the armchair. His head is back, his eyes are closed, and a small trickle of sweat makes its way down his forehead. He is breathing heavily, as if he has just run a race from which he is trying to recover. After a few minutes, his breathing returns to normal and he opens his eyes.

"Is that all?" says the boy.

"All?" says the grandfather. "Of course, it's not all. Life goes on."

In time, the memory of the giant and his daughter faded from the young man's memory, became the matter of a tale he would tell now and then in the great hall as the blind sage nodded knowingly from a corner. The son of the King of Ireland forgot the great fear and anxiety he had undergone, remembered only that he endured, survived, and came to believe his own wits had saved him. In the telling, the maiden, though she didn't disappear entirely, became peripheral to the plot, someone who stood by the sidelines, cheering him on, encouraging him, telling him he could do it if he tried. He was grateful for her help, but realized how foolish he had been to think he was in love with her. It had simply been a matter of propinquity.

When another year had passed, the King of Ireland proclaimed a marriage between his son and the daughter of the King of Denmark, to whom the boy had been betrothed since birth. People came from all over to join the celebration. A great feast was held at the castle. Boars were brought in and roasted on spits. Servants carried in trays laden with all sorts of fruits, breads, and pastries. There were jugglers, tumblers, and magicians. The King of Ireland sang a song, the King of Denmark told a tale, and the son of the King of Ireland played upon his golden harp. All present remarked that his was the sweetest music they had ever heard.

In the midst of all this merriment, through the casement window flew a golden falcon, which alighted on the floor. Scarcely had the bird touched the stones when there was a flash of light, and there before the multitude stood the giant's daughter, her golden tresses shining. She hobbled toward the great table and bowed low before the King of Ireland and the King of Denmark, then turned to the son of the King of Ireland.

"How are you thriving, Ireland's son?"

"I...I thrive very well, indeed."

"You did not thrive so well the day I cleaned that stable."

"I remember that," he said, fearful that she had come for his head.

"And you did not thrive so well the day I thatched the stable with birds' feathers, no two of the same kind or color. Nor the day you used my bones to climb the glass tree. Do you remember that?"

"Yes, I remember."

"And do your guests know the story?"

"Well," said the young man, "not exactly."

"I didn't think so," she said.

"Look, what do you want?"

"You made a promise to me the day I became lame and saved your head, do you remember?"

The young man shuddered. A promise. He had left the promise out of his tale in its many retellings, hoping it would be forgotten. But now there was no denying it.

"Y-yes," was all he could say.

"Then speak that promise to your guests."

"I promised," the youth began, swallowing the dryness in his throat, "to give you whatever you asked in return for your help."

"I now ask, before all this assembly, that you keep your bargain freely."

The young man lowered his eyes, and wishing for all the world that he could be somewhere else, whispered, "What do you seek?"

"That you acknowledge me as your wife."

The halls were filled with silence.

"But you are lame," he protested. "I cannot have a lame wife."

He looked at the King of Denmark, but the King of Denmark stared down at the table. He sought his father's eyes, but his father merely said, "Did you make this promise?"

"Yes," he answered.

"Never make promises you don't intend to keep," said the King.

He turned to the daughter of the King of Denmark, but she had turned her face away and was weeping softly into a handkerchief.

All eyes were upon him. The walls of the great hall, indeed, the entire universe seemed to rush at him as if their very existence depended upon his response. He felt trapped, bound in the web of his own duplicity, his failure to see things clearly, to admit his own deceptions. But as his eyes met those of the giant's daughter, he became aware that she had no hold on him. Should he deny her, nothing would happen. She would simply depart as if she had never been there. He would still have his head and, in years hereafter, inherit the throne of Ireland. The world would not change one jot. The choice was up to him.

Again he looked at the giant's daughter. At first, all he could see was the withered leg, the result of his own haste and carelessness, her pallid complexion, the bruised circles of her eyes. In his mind, she hobbled from room to room in the castle, leading behind her the deformed progeny of Ireland. But gradually he recalled the day he had first seen her, the lake of silver and her golden hair, and the love he had felt for her in that instant. He recalled the great sacrifice she had made for him, the blood that had washed over his hands and shirt, the bone that remained forever grafted to a tree of glass. And in that moment he named himself small and insignificant, a creature more deformed than the maiden could ever be.

The son of the King of Ireland stood straight before the assembly and gestured toward the ravaged maiden, his hand trembling, his heart fearful and uncertain of what the future held. "This is my true bride," he announced. "I will have her as my wife, and no other woman."

The assembled guests murmured and grumbled among themselves as the son of the King of Ireland stepped from the dais and led the giant's daughter hobbling from the hall.

The following morning, the son of the King of Ireland married the daughter of the giant of Killarney, and they lived a long life, though whether they were happy the tale does not tell. And their offspring endure to this very day.

The old man slumps back into his chair, eyes closed, face ruddy, exhausted, and triumphant. The boy knits his brow, puzzling over the tale he has just heard, and after a long moment, says to his grandfather, "I don't get it."

"Don't get it?" said the old man, sitting up to reach for his pipe. "What do you mean?"

"What's the point?"

"Point?"

"The message. The lesson."

"There's no message. No lesson. It's a story. That's the point," says the old man, furiously tamping tobacco into his pipe. "Listen here," he continues. "I learned that story from my grandfather. And he learned it from his grandfather before him. And where he learned it from, I can't say. But that's what stories are for. They're a kind of...a kind of...gift."

"Oh."

The boy stands and ambles toward the window, absentmindedly shuffling the cards in his hands. The day is grey, storm clouds gather in the sky, and the boy's head is filled with images of giants, golden harps and golden horns, a tree of glass, and a maiden with golden hair whose blood washes over the hands of a handsome prince.

It starts to rain.

He turns to his grandfather, ready to ask another question. But the old man's eyes are closed, and he is already snoring lightly, dreaming, most likely, of a tree on a high hillside.

First Kill

Jackie Jordan passed through dreams of dismemberment into darkness. Shadows moved. He held his breath and waited for the blond assassin to step once again from the shadow world as he had several months ago, grin as wide as the moon, dagger poised to plunge, perhaps conjured by the wail of sirens that pierced the morning to summon the battalion to alert, or perhaps by bursts of artillery that rumbled across the DMZ through the night. Whatever had conjured him, he appeared nightly to stand watch over Jackie's dreams, eyes ablaze, knife at the ready, given shape and substance by Jackie's abiding fear that some morning the sirens would announce a real invasion, the artillery's thunder call down a rain of blood, flesh, and fire.

Suddenly, he was there, his smile with teeth like nails. Jackie tried to move, but it was like swimming through molasses, and the smiler with the knife glided forward. The knife hovered above him, then descended slowly, oh, so slowly. He tried to yell, to scream something, but the knife kept coming. As it pricked his chest, he forced his eyes to open.

"Wake up, buddy. Wake up. 'S only me."

The blond assassin dissolved into dreams, and was replaced by George Tharp's face, front tooth broken, hair like a haystack.

Jackie swallowed and caught his breath.

"I'm okay now."

"Sure?"

"Sure."

"'Nother one a them dreams?"

"Yeah."

"Don' pay 'em no mine. They only in yer head."

Tharp stood up and grinned down. Jackie shook the last vestiges of dream from his head, rolled out of his bunk, and sat on the edge, contemplating his feet.

"Better get a move on," Tharp said. "'S almost time to go to the Zone."

"I'm coming," said Jackie. He padded into the latrine, slapped some cold water onto his face, and studied his reflection in the mirror, half expecting to see the dream assassin lurking in one of the stalls. His eyes were rimmed in red and his yellow hair hung down in gobs.

He didn't want to go to the Zone. He just wanted to get out of here without getting his ass shot off. He was glad they'd sent him here instead of to Vietnam, where they were sending all his friends. Jay and Pat were already there. He hadn't heard from them in months and was afraid something might have happened to them. Rick was in training and would be in Nam in a few weeks.

Korea was supposed to be safe. There wasn't supposed to be a war here. But scarcely more than a month ago, a North Korean patrol had crossed the Zone and killed three kids, the oldest nineteen, shot them in the face, mutilated their bodies, and stolen their dog tags so they couldn't be identified. Protests were lodged at Panmunjom and vigorously denied, and the entire affair became another "incident," not even important enough to be reported in the *Stars and Stripes*. That's when the dreams started, dreams in which he watched himself dismantled one piece at a time—an arm here, a leg there—until nothing remained. It was as if a disembodied force was scavenging body parts to construct something new and monstrous that would walk like Jackie and talk like Jackie, but would wander the world soulless.

Jackie began to wish he'd gone to Nam. At least you knew where you stood there.

"It's not just that I'm afraid to die," he'd told Tharp once. "It's that I don't want to kill anyone. I'm not a killer."

Tharp listened as he always did, his face attentive and stupid as an old hound dog's. It was one of those things Jackie liked about Tharp, his willingness to listen and not to judge, even if he didn't understand a word you said. But he'd wanted Tharp to understand.

"When I was ten years old, my father bought me a rifle and took me out hunting with him. I didn't want to go, but he said, 'Do you want to be a sissy all your life?' So I went.

"We'd been in the woods a couple of hours when we came upon this rabbit just sitting there minding its own business. My father pointed to him and said, 'There he is, Jackie. Get him.'

"I stood there watching that rabbit nibble on some leaves, sighting down the barrel of the rifle, but I couldn't shoot. My knees shook and I was sweating. Finally, my father got angry and growled at me, 'Damn it, boy. Shoot the son of a bitch.'

"So I closed my eyes and pulled the trigger. The blast knocked me right on my ass, and the rifle must have hit me because I could feel the blood running down my nose.

"'Jesus, Lord,' my father yelled. 'You got him first shot, Jackie. You got your first kill.'

"I got him, all right. Blasted his head right off. Blood and guts were everywhere, and I got sick. Ran right into the bushes and threw up. Later on, I cried all the way home.

"He didn't say anything to me the whole way home. But he said to my mother, 'It's all your fault. You're making a pansy out of the boy.'

"She didn't answer him. She just sat there pulling the needle through a pair of his pants she was working on so he'd have something to wear to work the next day. He never took me with him again."

When Jackie finished the story, Tharp sat grinning as if Jackie had given him a present.

"That was a nice story," he said.

Jackie knew he shouldn't have told the story.

"I just don't want to kill anyone," he insisted.

"Don't matter. Yer still m'friend."

Standing in front of the mirror, Jackie wished he could take the story back. He had let Tharp have too much of himself.

He padded back to his bunk and started dressing. Tharp already had his gear on and was sliding the bolt of the M-14 back and forth.

"Shore wish I had me one a them M-16s like they got in Vietnam," he said.

While Jackie dressed, Tharp prattled on about killing "gooks" and "gettin' inta some action." Tharp wasn't the kind of person Jackie would ordinarily choose as a friend. In fact, the friendship started as an accident.

Tharp had received a letter from the jewelry store where he bought Tina's diamond on credit. The store wanted him to return the diamond because he'd missed the last three payments. They called Tina and threatened to send the sheriff out to get the diamond. She was pissed at him and he just didn't know what to do.

Tharp tried writing them a letter, but when Jackie looked at it, he knew Tharp was digging himself in deeper. It was written so badly Jackie couldn't figure out what Tharp was trying to say, and almost every word was misspelled. Diamond was spelled "dimin," and money was spelled "mony." Tharp had even spelled his own name "Geoge" and had to go back and insert the missing "r."

"Let me help you out, George," Jackie said to him.

So they sat down together and worked out a plan to pay back the jewelry store. Tharp would send fifty dollars with the letter as a good faith gesture, and thirty dollars every month until the bill was paid off.

"I'm gonna come to you every payday," said Jackie, "and we'll go right to the bank and get a money order and send it right off."

They sent off the letter and the first money order, and a few weeks later, Tharp received a letter from the jewelry store saying everything was all right. Tharp was so happy when he read the letter he started to cry, then threw his arms around Jackie and hugged him.

"Goddamn, Jackie. I just 'preciate the hell outta what you done for me."

Jackie was embarrassed by this outburst of affection, especially when the other guys in the platoon burst into laughter and asked when the engagement was.

A few days later, Jackie received a letter from Tina, thanking him for what he'd done and inviting him to visit her and George when he got back to the States. "Your like family now," she'd written. She had also enclosed a photo of herself and inscribed it "To Jackie Love Tina" across the bottom. It wasn't a picture of her naked, thank God, but she was wearing this skimpy little two-piece bathing suit, and Jackie decided he wouldn't show Tharp the picture.

That night, as they sat around the barracks playing gin rummy and listening to Armed Forces Radio, Jackie was surprised to hear the disk jockey announce, "And this next one goes out to Spec.4 Jackie Jordan up there in the DMZ from Tina. Lucky dog, Jackie." They played "Hey Good Lookin'" by Hank Williams, and Tharp thought it was a howl.

"Was you surprised?" he asked.

Surprised wasn't the word. Stupefied was more like it.

But there was something disarming about Tharp's simplicity, and although Jackie didn't like to hear him talk about "killin' gooks," on the whole he considered Tharp a basically decent person. All Tharp's talk about violence was not really part of his nature. He didn't hate the North Koreans—he didn't hate anyone, for that matter—and he didn't consider killing them part of his patriotic duty. But he knew, without being able to articulate it, that this would be the only opportunity for glory he would ever have in his life.

Jackie felt sorry for Tharp, and a little guilty, knowing Tharp had invested so much in a friendship that could not possibly extend beyond their tour of duty. And he resented Tharp, too, for the commitment Tharp had, in all innocence, forced upon him. It had happened the night before the company headed up to the Zone, right after the three kids had been killed. They were sitting in the E.M. club by themselves drinking a few beers when Tharp reached across the table and plucked him by the sleeve.

"Jackie," he said, his face a little pale. "You gotta promise me sump'm."

"What's that, George?"

"If anythin' happens to me, you gotta write to Tina. Don't nobody else can tell her 'cept you."

"Nothing's going to happen."

"Happened to them boys."

"A fluke," said Jackie. "It's not going to happen again."

But Tharp insisted. "Just in case."

Jackie didn't want to do it, didn't think he could, but those hound dog eyes of Tharp's looked so sad he would have felt like a traitor if he'd said anything else. So he made the promise.

"Damn Tharp," he said, lacing up his boot.

"Whatcha thinkin', buddy?" Tharp said.

"Nothing."

"That ole dream still worryin' yer?"

"No. Just getting bored sitting in a foxhole every night."

"No sweat-ee-da. Two more days we be back at battalion."

"Thank Christ."

Jackie checked his rifle and headed out for formation.

The lieutenant had set up two stakes with phosphorescent tape at the ends outside the foxhole and told Jordan and Tharp, as he did every night, that if they had to fire, to fire between the two stakes. Jackie hadn't had to fire since they'd been in the Zone and hoped he wouldn't have to, but Tharp fired at everything that moved. Deer. Foxes. Raccoons. "Never know when it might be a gook," he said.

The foxhole was beginning to stink. Tharp stank, too. He hadn't bathed in about four days, but Jackie didn't want to say anything to hurt his feelings.

They spent most of the night in silence, since any noise might give away their position. Jackie stared at the stakes until the phosphorescent glow looked like a pair of eyes. He tried to think of something pleasant to keep the hours from bearing down on him. He thought of Becky, the girl he had broken up with before he came over, but the thought depressed him. They were supposed to marry when he came home, but those plans fell through the night he told her he wasn't going to work for her father. They argued, she cried, and as he watched her he saw that any marriage would have been a three-way affair, with her father as the linchpin. Still, he missed her more than he thought possible. Gradually, thoughts of Becky were pushed away by the dream assassin's smile, and he knew he was dozing.

"Want some?" said Tharp, handing him a plug of tobacco he always carried, shocking Jackie awake.

"No thanks." He'd never gotten used to chewing tobacco.

"Suit y'self," Tharp said, looking back out toward the stakes. A few minutes later he started giggling to himself.

"Know what I'm thinkin'?"

"No," Jackie answered. "What?"

"Tina," he said. "She's got the biggest, softest tits you ever see. I like to put m' face between 'em and go brrr," he said, closing his eyes and shaking his head like a wet spaniel. "You ever done that?"

"No, I haven't," Jackie said. He had avoided telling Tharp he was a virgin by making up a variety of stories, but he didn't want to tell stories or lies to him tonight.

"Ain't nothin' like it, Jackie. Ain't nothin' like it," Tharp said, spitting out a gob of tobacco juice that landed with a splat at the bottom of the foxhole.

Tharp was telling the truth about Tina. Jackie remembered the photo she had sent him, and Tharp had once shown Jackie a picture he had taken of her naked. Jackie agreed she had the largest breasts he had ever seen in his life. He told Tharp he was crazy to go around showing her picture to people that way, but to Tharp it was the most natural thing in the world. Her breasts, thought Jackie, were about the only thing she had going for her. Her face was ugly as hell, with pockmarks all over it, and her legs were so thin it was a wonder she could stand up on them. Jackie wondered what she was like, if she was as simple as Tharp.

"I writ her today, said we could get married when I get home. Have our honeymoon in Memphis, see can we spot Elvis."

Jackie congratulated Tharp and said he would buy him a drink when they got back to the battalion. Then he turned back to watch the stakes.

It was quiet for a long time except for the squishing of Tharp chewing his tobacco and the buzzing of insects. Jackie swatted at a few mosquitoes. Before long the sickle smile of the dream assassin told him he was dozing again. Suddenly Tharp hissed at him.

"Psst. Jackie. C'mere."

Jackie shook himself awake. "What is it?"

"You hear sump'm?"

He listened, but could hear only the sound of the insects.

"I don't hear anything. Maybe a deer."

"Sump'm out there. Listen."

Before Jackie could do anything, a flare went up and turned the night a bright silver. Five or six shapes scurried toward them like enormous rodents.

"Yahoo," yelled Tharp, and started firing. "I'm gonna get me one a them suckers."

The flare died out and Jackie found himself in total darkness. He cursed himself for not covering his eyes when the flare went off. His knees trembled and his arms felt as if the bones had been taken from them, but he managed to pull the trigger, swinging his rifle from the stake on the left to the stake on the right, keeping his shots low, hoping the firefight would be over soon. Tracers from the flanking foxholes zipped out in front of him like miniature comets.

Without warning, an explosion slammed him against the back of the foxhole. The rifle fell from his hands. Dirt and bits of metal showered down on him like hard rain, and he felt something stab his left shoulder. Everything began to look fuzzy.

"Shit," cried Tharp, and Jackie could hear the tears in his voice. Then Tharp began to groan. Jackie shook the fuzziness from his head and tried to focus on Tharp. Tharp was pressed against the back of the foxhole trying to push himself up with one hand and lift his rifle with the other. Blood was streaming down his face like gravy, and he was obviously terrified.

Jackie looked up toward the edge of the foxhole to see a black shadow looming over him like some prehistoric monolith. The shadow was pointing something at Tharp. Before Jackie identified the weapon, he heard three shots and Tharp's face was gone. The shadow swung around toward Jackie, eyes shining like fire, and Jackie found himself looking down the barrel of a rifle. The mouth of the rifle gaped at him, grew larger and larger as if it were going to swallow him.

Then it clicked.

When it clicked a second time, Jackie knew that the shadow had run out of ammunition. He swung his rifle up and pulled the trigger, but it jammed. The blade of a knife gleamed above the foxhole, hovering over him until the night was gone and there was only the blade descending.

He leaped to his feet and, wielding his rifle like a club, the pain in his shoulder dulled by his rage to live, cracked the shadow's kneecap with the butt and sent him sprawling. By the time Jackie scrambled out of the foxhole, the North Korean was on his feet again, his knife arm raised. Jackie jammed the rifle butt into the Korean's chest and sent him tumbling backwards, but the Korean came at him again.

"Jesus Christ," Jackie cried, shuddering. "Stay down, goddammit. STAY DOWN."

All he could see was the knife lunging at him and a sudden vision of himself slit up the middle like a gutted chicken, and Tharp's face blasted to twitching meat. Again he swung at the Korean, this time catching him at the side of the head. The Korean went down and the knife went flying. The Korean rolled over to reach for it, and Jackie brought his boot down hard on the man's wrist and hit him in the face again with the rifle butt, but the Korean still kept trying to get up.

Jackie's actions were automatic now. He kept pounding at the man's head, over and over and over in an ecstasy of rage, until the man stopped moving and his face was bloody and raw like hamburger; then he stopped.

Jackie looked down at the man, trying to suck in lung full after lung full of air. He'd never worked so hard in his life. His chest hurt. There were no features left to the man's face, just blood and meat and what might have been the remnant of a nose, but Jackie was aware the man he had killed was just a kid, like Tharp with his face gone, like the rabbit whose head he had blown off.

When the lieutenant found him, Jackie was kneeling over the dead man, crying and choking out "Jesus, God. Jesus, God," like a child who had just been beaten. The lieutenant touched him on the shoulder and whispered, "It's okay, Jordan. It's over now," the same way his mother used to whisper when he'd hurt himself.

Jackie looked up and past the lieutenant at the stars as if he expected them to strike him dead.

Jackie hadn't been wounded seriously enough to be sent home, just sent to the hospital for a few days. The lieutenant came in to see him a couple of times.

"How you feeling, Jordan?"

"Feeling okay, I guess."

The lieutenant pulled up a chair and straddled it, his arms folded across the backrest.

"Everybody at the company says hi and hopes you'll be back soon."

"That's nice." Jackie didn't feel like talking, and didn't want to go back to the company.

"I put you in for a Purple Heart, couple of other medals, too. You deserve 'em. You're a hero, you know."

Jackie didn't say anything, just nodded and looked down at his hands. They were covered with cuts and abrasions and hurt like hell.

"Oh, by the way," said the lieutenant, pulling a yellow envelope from his breast pocket. He unfolded it and handed it to Jackie.

"This came for you. We called your folks to let them know. You ought to call them, tell them you're all right."

It was a telegram from his father. His father was proud of him, called him a hero. Jackie knew he was supposed to feel good about that, but somehow it didn't seem to matter. He didn't know how a hero was supposed to feel, but if it felt like what he felt now, he didn't want to be a hero. As far as he could see, a hero was only someone who had lost some piece of himself and managed not to die. Tharp and the North Korean were not heroes.

After the lieutenant left, Jackie started to write the letter to Tina as he had promised Tharp.

He started, "Dear Tina: I'm sorry about George," but couldn't write any more. He couldn't tell her what it was like to watch Tharp die. He couldn't tell her that it was Tharp who gave away their position by firing too soon, and that's why he died. He wanted to tell her Tharp was a hero, that he'd saved Jackie's life. Maybe she'd get some consolation from that. But he couldn't tell that easy lie. He'd already lost enough of himself in the Zone. He'd write to her some other time, tell her the truth some other time, when things didn't hurt so much, just so she'd know.

Consecration

Father Raymond Salko stared past the wafer of bread, not knowing what it was or what he was supposed to do with it. The paralysis lasted no more than a few seconds, and perhaps no one noticed, but to him it seemed as if he had stepped into a universe where nothing was familiar, where there were only things and no names. Faces watched in silence, waiting for him to utter the words that would speak them from their stillness. He struggled up through himself, past the faces, past the eyes, and focused on the wafer, the communion host, the cross stamped on its surface, until, with neither relief nor conviction, the words came, and he said them as if they were the only and most terrifying words that had ever been spoken: "This is my body."

As he lowered the host, someone he had never seen before—a bearded man in an army field jacket—rose and slipped out the side door.

Later, in the sacristy, Father Salko removed his vestments in silence and hung them in the closet. He turned to find himself facing Rose Anderson. She twisted a tissue in her hands as she had every Saturday evening for the last six months.

"He's still drinking, Father. What am I supposed to do?"

She had said the same thing for six months.

Father Salko embraced Rose, and she sobbed against his chest. This, too, had become a ritual, one he had established to insulate himself against her. He was especially susceptible to a woman's tears, and as Rose wept, desire awakened within him. He had always suspected she came to him not only for spiritual counseling or the strength of Christ to help her endure what had become, as far as he could see, a truly loveless and perhaps even violent marriage, but because she was physically attracted to him (though she probably didn't realize this herself) and received from him the warmth and affection she did not receive at home. Suspecting all this, and knowing the urges that stirred within him, he insulated himself with ritual—and by gently insisting that she continue to address him as "Father" rather than "Ray."

"Rose," he said, gently pushing her away from him. "You know you can't stop him from drinking."

He paused. He wanted to shake her. He'd been telling her this for the last six months, too. He stared at the wet blueness of her eyes, felt it tug at him, urge him to place his mouth against hers.

He rushed on. "He's a sick man and needs professional help. You have to accept that. You need help, too. Help I can't give you. You need to talk to people who have been through this and found out how to cope with it."

He dropped his hands from her shoulders and turned away from her toward his desk.

"Father, I'm afraid," she said.

"We're all afraid." He thumbed through his file of telephone numbers to avoid looking at her, afraid that she would say or do something to break through the wall of compassion that guarded his celibacy. "That's why we pray, to ask God to walk with us in our fear."

He drew a card from the file and copied the phone number onto a sheet of memo pad.

"Call this number," he said. "Someone will call you back, talk to you, maybe even take you to a meeting."

"What is this?"

"It's a group made up of people like you, people with problem drinkers in their families."

She looked at the piece of paper, then at him as if he had just rejected her. "I don't know," she said.

"It will help. I promise."

After she left, Raymond Salko knelt at the side altar, his forehead propped against his folded hands, his eyes closed. He tried to pray, but tonight there were no prayers in him. Instead, he was filled with failure. Six months and Rose was still in pain. Her husband Ed was still drinking, still sleeping around with God knew how many women, throwing his money around, avoiding his wife and two sons. Six months, and nothing Raymond Salko had done had made a difference.

In the thirty years he had been a priest, what had he accomplished? The Andersons were the least of his failures. Since he had been pastor at St. Cecilia's—seven years, now—church attendance had declined steadily, the school had closed. Vandalism had forced him to close the church nightly from eight o'clock on and to place bars and screening over the stained glass windows. And now, after what had happened during mass, he felt as if the very core of what he believed was slipping away from him.

He locked the church for the night, then circled the grounds once, checking every door and window to make sure it was securely fastened. Snow was forecast, with temperatures in single digits. He mounted the steps of the rectory, opened the door, and a sudden chill swept through him. The faint scent of Father Boland's port drifted through the hallway, though the former pastor died nine years ago. The odor of fish that Father Firling, drowned in a boating accident three years ago, brought back from his Saturday outings still permeated the kitchen. It was like living among the souls of the dead, though in his more rational moments Father Salko knew that these fragrances were mere tricks of memory, olfactory hallucinations. Nevertheless, the rectory, too, was growing strange and unfamiliar, a place where he could not recall the names of things

He heated some stew left from last night's dinner and ate in silence. When he finished, he washed his plate and put the uneaten stew in the refrigerator. Enough remained for one more good meal. Then he made his way to the study to work on next week's homily.

He poured a glass of sherry, lit his pipe, and wrote, "Even Christ had doubts, moments when the insistence of the flesh struggled against the God within." He thought of Rose, her wet blue eyes, the freckles that bridged her nose, the silky brown hair with a few strands of gray, and wondered if Christ had thought about Mary Magdalene the same way. He continued: "In Gethsemane He pleaded that the cup of His death be removed. On the cross, every atom of His humanity cried out, 'Father, why have you forsaken me?' If Christ had doubts, how can we expect more from ourselves?"

The doorbell buzzed.

Raymond Salko put his notebook aside, set his pipe, bowl down, in the ashtray, and went to the front door. At first he couldn't see who was standing in the shadow of the porch, but when the figure moved into the light, he recognized the stranger from church. The man stood with his bare hands half inside the pockets of an army field jacket, Vietnam era, from which the insignia had been removed, moving his arms slightly as if they were wings.

"Good evening. Something I can help you with?" asked the priest.

The stranger's eyes were dark, deep, the irises round and blank as nail heads.

"I saw your light," said the stranger. "Are you busy?"

"I'm afraid I am busy at the moment."

The stranger's arms stopped moving. "I won't take long, Father. I just want to talk is all."

The priest was about to close the door on the man, about to tell him to come back tomorrow, but remembered that he was a priest. "Please come in," he said.

He stepped back so the man could enter, then closed the door behind him.

Though the stranger affected the clothing of someone much younger—red and black checked wool shirt, jeans, and sneakers—it was clear from the strands of gray among his deep brown hair and beard, the wrinkles about his eyes and mouth, that he was probably in his late forties, perhaps early fifties, about the priest's age, though whether he was older or younger was hard to tell. He wore a blue backpack with red trim strapped to his back.

The stranger studied the dark wood of the hallway, the moldings, the stairway.

"Nice place. You live by yourself?"

"Quite," the priest answered. "The bishop hasn't seen fit to send me an assistant."

"Too bad."

There was a silence.

"Would you care to sit down, Mr.?..."

"Oh. Yeah. Chandler. Emmett Chandler."

"I'm Raymond Salko." He guided Chandler into the study and gestured toward an easy chair.

Chandler shrugged out of his backpack and flopped into the chair.

"Okay if I smoke?"

"Help yourself."

He drew a pack of Camels from his jacket pocket and shook a cigarette from the pack, tapping it against the back of his hand before lighting it.

"This is a great study. All that exposed wood. You keep it up yourself?"

"I do what I can."

Chandler's eyes moved slowly across the room, registering everything, nailing it into place: the oak bookcases, the statue of the Virgin in the corner, the writing desk near the window, the Oriental rug on the floor.

"How may I help you, Mr. Chandler?"

"What?"

"You said you needed help."

"Did I say that? No, I don't need help."

"The Sacrament of Reconciliation?"

"The what?"

"Confession."

"Is that what they call it now? No, no, nothing like that. It's just that I've been away a long time and came back to see some people I knew, visit the old places. This is one of the places."

Father Salko was relieved. For a brief moment, he feared that Chandler wanted something from him, needed something—spiritual guidance, advice, consolation of some sort. And tonight, he didn't have the energy.

"Would you care for something to drink? Tea? Coffee? I may even have some soda in the refrigerator."

"No thanks."

"Something to eat, then? You look hungry."

"No, really. I'm fine."

Chandler's eyes kept darting around the room, and he fidgeted with his cigarette, rolling it around in his fingers, flicking the ashes into the ashtray.

"I'm a Catholic. Was a Catholic. Used to be an altar boy, too, right here at Saint Cecilia's. Served mass for Father Maguire—did you know him?—a couple of times a week. I'd get up at six o'clock in the morning, get dressed in the dark, and walk the two or three blocks to church. I'd be the first one there. I'd be there a long time before Father Maguire, or the Monsignor, or whoever was saying mass that morning.

"I liked being there when the church was all dark, especially in winter when there was snow on the ground and it was cold outside, because it was warm inside and you could feel safe. I liked sitting in the sanctuary with no lights on, just the sanctuary candle burning inside its red glass shield, and maybe a couple of devotional candles flickering at the side altars. It felt holy there, like God was all around and you'd never have to worry about anything.

"I was a good altar boy, too. Knew all the prayers by heart, and even to this day can remember most of them. *Introibo ad altare Dei. Ad deum qui laetificat juventutem meam.* I could say them as fast as you want, because Father McGuire used to speed through them and all the words would run together like so many boxcars.

"*Introiboadaltaredeiaddeumquilaetificatjuventutemmeam,* just like that."

"It came from going to a Catholic school. My parents sent me to Saint Cecilia's because they thought I'd get a good education, and because it had better discipline than the public schools. Not that my parents were very good Catholics. Fact is, they hardly went to church at all.

"My favorite teacher was Sister Augustine. She used to tell us all kinds of stories, mostly about the communists and how they persecuted Catholics in Russia and other iron curtain countries. The one I remember most was about a man who lived in Poland or Yugoslavia or one of those places. He didn't believe in God and wanted to show this Catholic boy that there was no God, so he asked the boy to steal a communion host. Said he wanted to receive communion, but they wouldn't let him because he was a communist.

"The boy stole the host and gave it to the man, but instead of eating it, the man took a long needle and stuck it through the host. The host started to bleed. It bled all over the man's hands and dripped on the floor, Sister said. He'd never seen so much blood in his life. The man was so scared, the next day he went to the priest and was baptized. Sister said he began to speak out against the communists and was finally killed by them—'granted a martyr's death,' was the phrase she used."

Father Salko remembered the story, or one very much like it. Even then, he had considered it preposterous, like the tales of Jews ritually murdering Christian children. He was about to say as much, but thought better of it and allowed Chandler to continue.

"I kept thinking about that story. I even dreamed about it, blood flowing out of the bread until it covered the world. Every time I served mass, I could hardly keep from trembling whenever the priest placed the host on my tongue, terrified that I might break it or accidentally bite it, and the blood would come tumbling from my lips, and the priest would know what a horrible sinner I was.

"Then one morning I was serving for Monsignor Cassidy. He was a very old man, maybe in his eighties or nineties, and going blind. He wore these thick glasses, and I would lead him out to the altar with his hand on my shoulder. He was so arthritic he couldn't genuflect, only dip his knee a bit. And his hands shook so, I was afraid he would drop something.

"I served for him once a week, a private mass in the main church upstairs because he couldn't manage the stairs to the downstairs chapel where they held the daily masses. He'd say mass at the side altar, the Virgin's altar, and the only lights would be the exit light by the side door and the candles I lit before mass. I don't know how he managed to read from the book to say all the prayers, but he did.

"On this one morning, right after the consecration, after he had divided the host, he dropped a piece of it on the floor. Then he stepped on it, accidentally, of course, crushed it under his heel.

"'Monsignor,' I cried out. 'The host.'

"'Eh?' he said.

"'You dropped the host.'

"He looked bewildered, confused. His head bobbed up and down, back and forth.

"'Don't stand there, lad,' he said. 'Pick it up.'

"I was horrified. What he wanted me to do was sacrilegious.

"'Here,' he said, handing me a handkerchief he had taken from his sleeve. 'Put it in this.'

"I tried to pick up the pieces with the handkerchief, but couldn't get them all, so I used my hands. I was shaking, afraid that I would be struck dead. But nothing happened. Afterwards, in the sacristy when I had finished helping him out of his vestments, I asked him for absolution.

"'Absolution?' he said.

"'I touched the host.'

"'Yes, thank you.'

"'With my bare hands. I couldn't get it all with the cloth.'

"'You're a good lad.'

"'But it's a sin, monsignor.'

"He gave me a strange look as if I had just said something preposterous, then nodded.

"'A sin to touch the Lord's body? What an idea.'

"'But...'

"He gestured the sign of the cross at me, then muttered, 'It's all right, lad. Off to school with you.'"

Chandler stared at his hands as if flecks of dust from the communion wafer still cling to his fingers.

Father Salko hadn't thought about Monsignor Cassidy in years, but Chandler's story had unlocked an image, his last memory of the man, a most chilling one. He and Father Johanssen had gone to the rest home to bring the Monsignor the Eucharist. They found the old priest seated in his room, pale and wasted, almost ghostly, his hands folded, thumbs and forefingers brought together holding an invisible wafer, his head bowed, whispering at his hands, "*Hoc est enim corpus meum.*" Then he closed his eyes, brought his hands to his lips, placed the invisible wafer in his mouth, and chewed. He kept doing the same thing, over and over.

"His mind is gone," Father Johanssen had said.

But Father Salko had wondered. Was this consecration of air a sign of the old priest's final lapse into mindlessness? Or had he achieved the ultimate lucidity? Was it mindlessness, the body responding automatically and habitually to the electrical impulses of a decaying brain? Or had the old man, on his journey inward, his final approach to death's gate, reached some revelation that the very air could be transformed by a simple puff of breath and five words in an archaic language, five words that could renew the face of the earth?

The image had haunted Raymond Salko in his early years as a priest, and had returned, after all this time, to haunt him once again.

Chandler continued.

"I didn't know what to think. Nothing had happened. My hands didn't burn, didn't grow paralyzed or leprous, and the Monsignor didn't seem to think it was important. Maybe there was nothing more there than bread. Maybe it was just another story, like Santa Claus. I thought about it, and the next week when I served mass for him, I took the host from my mouth when his back was turned and put it in an envelope I had brought with me. All day I sat in school with the host in my pocket, half fearful that the finger of God would point me out to the rest of the class. When I got home, I slipped it between the pages of *Treasure Island* before I went out to play.

"That night, after everyone had gone to bed, I locked my bedroom door, stuffed towels into the cracks so the light wouldn't shine through, turned on the table lamp, and took the host out of its envelope. In my palm, it looked and felt like a circle of paper, fluted around the edges where it had dried out. I stared at it for a long time. I was shaking, afraid that I was at the edge of damnation, but I knew that God, in his anger, would show himself to me and remove all my doubts.

"I took a needle and pushed it ever so slowly through the host. There was no blood, not a drop, just the hole the needle had made. Maybe I was doing it wrong. I took an Exacto blade from my modeling kit and drew it down the center of the wafer as if I were dissecting a frog, watching for the blood to flow, for something to happen. Nothing. Absolutely nothing. It was just bread.

"I began to cry, ashamed that I had been so easily fooled. It was a lie. Everything I had believed in was a lie. This wasn't Christ's body or anything else mysterious. It was just a bit of flour and water, cooked to dryness, that tasted like paste. My shame grew to rage, and I decided to get back at them all.

"So I grabbed a hammer, tiptoed out of the house, and made my way down to the church. It was open all night in those days, or at least the downstairs chapel. There was only a dim light in the vestibule, and one in the sanctuary, plus the sanctuary candle, a couple of vigil candles flickering in front of the statue of the Virgin. I took the hammer and pried open the door on the tabernacle where they kept the ciborium full of consecrated hosts. Then I grabbed a handful of hosts and stuffed them into my mouth, chewed them, swallowed them. They were dry as paper, and I nearly gagged on them a couple of times, but I kept stuffing them into my mouth, daring God to strike me down, until they were gone and all that remained were a few crumbs on the altar. Then I tossed the ciborium away and turned around. Nothing had changed. The vigil candles still flickered, the chapel was dark and empty. No hand of God had charged from a cloud to strike me dead, no demons appeared to carry me off. And I was aware that there was only me, me and things, that the world was just things."

Chandler fell silent. His eyes wandered along the dark wood of the molding along the ceiling as if to affirm the truth of what he had just said.

Father Salko quietly lifted his pipe from the ashtray, ran his thumb over the outer surface of the bowl, then placed it back in the ashtray. He was drowsy from the sherry, and his head was beginning to ache. It was only a matter of—what? God's grace? Cosmic coincidence?—that he was not sitting in Chandler's place, recounting his own lapse of faith to a priest he had never met before.

"They never found out who did it," said Chandler. "I didn't serve mass anymore after that, and when the year was over, I left St. Cecilia's and went to the public school."

The priest waited for him to continue, but Chandler said nothing. He merely fixed the priest with his gaze, his face gray and wasted.

Father Salko drained the remaining sherry from the glass and set the glass down on the table.

"That's a long time to be carrying this thing around, don't you think?"

"Carrying around?" said Chandler. "I'm not carrying anything. It's what happened is all."

"Oh," said the priest. "The incident doesn't still bother you?"

"No. It's just something that happened."

"Then why did you come here tonight?"

"No place else to go. I saw the light in the chapel and came in. I wanted to see if that changed, too. But I also wanted to look at someone who still believed, see what they looked like."

Chandler paused, turned his head away for a moment, then stared directly into Raymond Salko's eyes, those nail-head irises boring into the priest.

"But I didn't see anyone."

The priest held himself steady under Chandler's stare. There was no hostility in Chandler's eyes, no threat of scorn or violence. Instead there was a softness, a sadness, something the priest interpreted as compassion, tugging at him, drawing him in, pulling him down, behind which was simply a vast emptiness born of pain and loss. It was as if Chandler had discovered the hollowness at the center of the priest's heart, was about to strike him down, or worse, reveal his apostasy to the world.

"What do you want from me?" murmured the priest.

"Nothing," said Chandler. "Just a place to sit for a few minutes."

For a moment Raymond Salko was aware of the odor of Father Boland's port, a slight rush of wind sliding past the windows, the shadow of the Monsignor whispering against his folded hands.

Chandler leaned forward and rose from his chair. He put the cigarettes back into his pocket, then picked up the blue backpack and put his arms through the straps.

"I've got to go." Chandler zipped up the field jacket and pulled the black watch cap down over his ears.

The priest felt the need to say something, do something to make up for what had become of Chandler and for his own lack of faith, his own failure as a priest.

"Are you sure you won't try a little of that stew?" he said. "It won't take a minute to warm it up."

"Sorry, Ray. I've got a bus to catch."

He walked Chandler to the front door, and as he held it open, a gust of icy wind blew into the foyer.

"Gloves," said the priest. "You have no gloves."

He reached up to the shelf by the front door, took down a pair of dark brown gloves lined with rabbit fur.

"Take these," he said. "I have another pair."

Chandler looked down at the gloves, then at the priest.

"I don't need them."

Father Salko held the gloves up before Chandler's face, and placed them in his right hand.

"Your hands will get cold," was all the priest could think of.

Chandler hesitated, took the gloves, but did not put them on. He nodded once, then turned away into the night.

When he was gone, Father Salko returned to the study, and clicked off the table lamp. He felt himself fill with darkness. He thought again of Rose and wondered what he could give her, whatever could he possibly give her, that would make up for his earlier rebuke? What could he give anyone, for that matter? How terrifying it must have been to be Christ, to see the brokenness of the world, the depth of its pain, and to realize that no matter how many lepers he healed, how many blind men he made to see, how many times he had his body broken, it would never be finished.

He sipped at the sherry, momentarily distracted by its sudden sweetness. The first few flakes of snow snicked at the windowpane. He laid his head back and sat in the darkness as if anticipating a revelation, and contemplated the state of his own soul.

911

1

"Where are the kids? Have you got the kids?"
"Huh? The kids?"
"The kids, the kids. Aren't they with you?"
Bernie stared at his wife, then at the house, then back at her. "Where are the kids?" he said.

"You moron," she screeched, and slammed both fists against his chest, knocking him against the tree. "You fucking moron. You left them in the fucking house."

The tears burst from her eyes and she started running back toward the house.

That's when he heard the children screaming from the second floor and knew it had gone wrong. Flames shot from the front door. Sarah was dancing before the flames, ducking and dancing and trying to get in, but she couldn't get past.

He couldn't believe how quickly the fire had spread, didn't know fire could spread that fast. Smoke was already coming from the second story window. Sarah darted away from the front door and around toward the back, screaming, "Kimmy, Danny, Danny, Kimmy."

Bernie didn't know what to do next. Get help, maybe. He buried his hands deep in his pockets, as if he would find something there that would tell him what to do.

He ran next door to the Cannons and pounded on their door. Edgar Cannon came to the front door in a burgundy bathrobe, his graying hair disheveled.

"What the hell is going on?"

"I'm sorry to bother you, Mr. Cannon. But could you call the fire people? It's my house."

"Fire people? What are you talking about?"

"My kids. They're still in there."

Bernie pointed back to his house.

"Jesus Christ," said Cannon. "Margaret," he called over his shoulder. "Call 911. Tell them there's a fire. Now."

Then he pushed past Bernie and ran across the lawn toward the burning house, the burgundy bathrobe billowing out behind him.

Bernie was aware that his hands were once again buried deep in his pockets, looking for an answer, and that he hadn't budged from Cannon's porch. Cannon was trying to fight his way through Bernie's front door as Sarah had tried to a few moments before, but without much success. The flames pushed back like a giant's hands, denying him entry. Sarah came back from around the house and joined Cannon. The fire had burned holes in her nighty and he could see right through them. Patches of Cannon's bathrobe started to smolder where sparks had fallen on it. Bernie kept watching Cannon to make sure he didn't try anything funny with Sarah.

Bernie lit a cigarette to keep himself from panicking and started toward the house. The children weren't screaming anymore, but coming from the east there were sirens wailing and the bells of a fire truck clanging. He broke into a run to see if he could help Sarah and Cannon and lost the cigarette. Sarah and Cannon were backing away from the door as if they were being pushed. Bernie tried to push past them, but there seemed to be a wall there and he felt the backs of his hands burning and smelled burning hair, which he knew was his own.

He was ducking and weaving with his eyes closed because the heat was too much for him to open them and he knew they would boil right out of their sockets if he opened them, but he had to get the kids, find some way to get the kids or Sarah would hate him for the rest of her life, almost as much as he would hate himself.

In another instant, a pair of hands grabbed him and pulled him out of the way. There were voices yelling and shouting orders, and the sounds of engines, and Sarah screaming, "My kids are in there. Get my kids out."

He rubbed his eyes, tried to wipe the stinging out of them, and opened them just a slit. There were firemen running everywhere. They were unraveling hoses across his lawn, some of them were carrying axes. One ran toward him.

"Where are they?"

"Huh?"

"The kids, where are they?"

"In the house."

"Where in the house? Which room?"

"Upstairs bedroom."

"Point to it."

"On the left, up there."

Bernie pointed to the window where he'd last seen the kids.

"How many?"

"How many what?"

"Kids. How many kids are in there?"

"Two. Kimmy and Danny."

The fireman turned and started toward the house, beckoning toward someone behind Bernie. A hook and ladder truck was near the house, extending its ladder to the window where Bernie had just pointed.

2

"Can you tell me what happened, Mr. Carpenter?"

There were two cops. One of them was a lot shorter than Bernie, with dark curly hair, and it looked as if he hadn't even started shaving yet. He kept calling Bernie "sir." The other was a black guy, except that he didn't talk like any black guy Bernie had ever known or seen on TV, except a couple he'd seen on the news shows who were trying to talk like white men. This one didn't say "motherfucker" or "yo, dude" or anything like that. This one talked like a college professor, or what Bernie thought a college professor might sound like.

Bernie leaned his back against the police car and folded his arms as if he were hugging himself. He felt cold even though the air was warm. He kept his head down, looking at his shoes and the shoes of the cop who was asking him questions.

"I don't know."

They had put a coat around Sarah and bundled her off in the ambulance just after she had swung her fist into his face, giving him a bloody nose, and screamed, "You killed them, you motherfucker, you goddamned bastard." It had taken three of them to pull her away as she kicked at him and scratched at him with those long nails of hers. A few minutes earlier, they had put the kids' bodies into another ambulance and carried them away. At first he didn't know what was in the bags until the cop came up to him and ever so gently told him how sorry he was about the kids. Bernie'd just said, "Oh," and stared at the back of the ambulance before it had pulled away, because he didn't want to bust into tears in front of these two cops who would surely think he was a baby if he cried. It was just after the first ambulance had pulled away that Sarah had attacked him.

Now he was standing with blood all over his shirt where it had run down from his nose. His nose throbbed and he couldn't breathe and his cheeks stung where Sarah had dragged her nails down them.

"Where were you when the fire started, Bernie?" the black guy said. His name was Walker. The short one's name was Barrett. They hadn't said their first names.

"Me? I was...uh...outside having a cigarette."

"You know how the fire got started? Did you maybe leave a cigarette burning, drop a match, something like that?"

He knew what they were after. They wanted him to say that he'd started the fire. Then they'd say that he'd killed the kids, and that's not what he'd wanted. Not at all.

"I told you I don't know. I was outside having a cigarette."

The black guy was trying to get Bernie to look him in the eye, but Bernie wouldn't do it. The short guy was leaning one hand against the car looking at him. The black guy was standing in front of Bernie, tapping his pencil against a notebook.

"I know this has been tough on you, with your kids and all, but if you could just help us out a bit, help us understand how the fire got started, we could wrap this up tonight."

"I can't tell you anything. It's just that one minute I come out to have a cigarette, and the next minute the house is on fire. That's all I know. Can I go see my wife now?"

3

They stayed with Bernie's parents. They couldn't stay with Sarah's. Besides the fact that Sarah's parents had told her she could never come back, Sarah wouldn't have gone back even if they had wanted her to. They'd want her to start going to church again, and she couldn't stand that. That made Bernie sad, not because he was much of a Christian himself, but at least he believed in some kind of God. It made sense to believe in something.

So they stayed with his parents, even though he wasn't comfortable with them, either, especially his father. It wasn't that his father was an awful man—he wasn't. Wayne Carpenter never said much, just sat there most of the time watching the sports channel, or if there wasn't something interesting on the sports channel, flipping through the channels looking for something good. When he'd heard about the kids, he hadn't said much, just got this expression that pulled the lines of his face down, and went into the bathroom and closed the door. Bernie'd stood outside listening to the old man sob as if he were sucking in deep breaths, then bang his hand against the shower stall three times, and that was it. That's the way he'd always dealt with things. It's what he'd done when Bernie's grandparents had died. He'd gone into the bathroom, then come out an hour later as if nothing had happened and gone about what was necessary.

Bernie's mother had cried. In fact, she had wailed, had enfolded Sarah in her arms and let out with these large gulping sounds that made Bernie think of owls or whatever those birds were that made those sounds that kept you awake all night. And when she had finished holding Sarah, she flitted around the house still wailing, her arms flapping back and forth in front of her as if she were swatting away gnats, crying "Oh, those poor babies, those poor, poor babies."

Bernie sat at the kitchen table and smoked one cigarette after the other while the women wailed. He must have gone through a half a pack of cigarettes and a pot of coffee before his father came out of the bathroom and sat down across from him. He touched Bernie's shaking hand for a second or two, just to let him know how sorry he was, though he never said it, then withdrew the hand.

"What are you going to do now?" said Wayne Carpenter.

"I don't know."

"You made funeral arrangements?"

Funeral arrangements. Jesus, he hadn't even thought about funeral arrangements. He'd have to do that.

"No, pop. I didn't make any arrangements."

"I'll do it."

His father pushed himself away from the table and went into the living room to make the telephone call. Bernie lit another cigarette and stared out the window at the woods behind his father's house. His mother was still wailing in the bedroom and he couldn't hear Sarah, though he figured she must still be crying. He heard his father speaking in short phrases in the living room.

After a few minutes the telephone conversation stopped and Bernie waited. The television was still going. When he heard the staticky sound of channels being flipped, he realized his father wasn't coming back to the kitchen and that he would have to go into the living room.

Wayne Carpenter had his feet up on the La-Z-Boy and was aiming the remote control at the television set. Images flashed by on the screen: someone teeing off on a golf green; an ad for toilet bowl cleaner; a gigantic double cheeseburger with an oversized box of French fries; a couple kissing each other in bed, the sheet pulled up modestly above their chests; a game show displaying a large board of boxed letters that didn't quite make words behind a host with a wide, toothy smile. His father finally paused at the image of a white male and a coffee-colored female sitting behind a desk, a couple of sheets of paper in their hands. The top portion of the word "News" showed on the front panel of the desk.

"Quiet," said his father, "it's the news," as if Bernie didn't know.

Bernie knew enough not to address his father when the news was on, or when he was engrossed with anything else on television. So he sat back and watched the news with his father, the way they used to do, in silence. And as usual, just about everything on the news went past him. It wasn't as if he didn't understand what they were saying. He could do that well enough. But when they were done, he couldn't remember what they had said, or maybe just didn't consider it important enough to remember.

Now there was an image on television he would remember. It was Sarah being bundled into the back of an ambulance, a fireman's jacket draped over her shoulders. The next shot was of his house, engulfed in flames, spouts of water piercing the windows and a network of fire hoses crawling across the ground.

A woman stood in the foreground with a microphone in her hand after the fire had been put out. She was saying that "two children died in the blaze" and that the cause of the fire was "under investigation."

Just as the report ended, the telephone rang.

"Get that," his father said.

Bernie answered the phone and was surprised when the woman at the other end asked for him. She identified herself as someone from the newspaper, said she was sorry for his loss, and asked if he would mind answering a few questions. Bernie said, "No." She asked him things like what his full name was, where he was born, and what he did for a living. Then she asked him about the fire, if he knew how it got started, what he did while the fire was going on, and how he felt about the kids. He told her he didn't know how the fire got started, that he kept trying to get to the house but couldn't because of the heat and that he'd burned the backs of his hands and his eyebrows.

"I can't talk about the kids," he said. "Too hard."

The next question stopped him.

"Mr. Carpenter, why did your wife hit you?"

He didn't answer for a few seconds, didn't know what to answer. What was she trying to do?

"My wife didn't hit me."

"Someone saw her hit you," the woman said, "and then saw you a few minutes later with a bloody nose."

"She was upset," he said. "She didn't know what she was doing. She didn't connect."

"Then how did you get the bloody nose?"

"I don't know. I got it during the fire. Maybe I ran into something. Maybe it was the heat."

This time it was the woman who paused.

"Mr. Carpenter, I don't know how to say this." She stopped for about a half a breath. "There's a rumor going around that you set the fire. Is there any truth to that?"

Bernie rubbed his right hand up and down against his pants leg and felt his throat tighten. She was just like those cops. She was trying to get him to say that he had started the fire so they could blame him for his kids dying when it wasn't his fault.

"Who told you that?" he croaked into the phone.

"I can't tell you," the woman said. "Is it true?"

"No, it's not," he said. "It's a lie, and I'm not talking to you any more."

He banged the phone down so hard he expected his father to yell at him for trying to break it, but Wayne Carpenter was still staring fixedly at the image of the coffee-colored woman on the television screen, the remote control resting loosely in his hand.

Bernie went out to the front porch and lit a cigarette.

He'd been smoking a lot since the fire. The back of his throat burned from it and he noted the tell-tale yellow stains on his first two fingers, in spite of the burns. Maybe he'd give it up, quit. They said you could die from cancer or some other disease that filled up your lungs with fibers, like spiders were building their webs in them. But he needed to get through this day, just get through this one day. He'd finish up this one pack and wouldn't buy another. He'd do it for the sake of the k...

"Bernie?"

He turned around. Sarah stood in the doorway, her left hand holding the screen door half open. She looked like hell. Her eyes were crimson from crying, her eyebrows had been burned away and her hair was singed. Her face was red as if it had been sunburned and her hands were bandaged.

"You okay?" he said.

Her face hardened and she slammed the screen door behind her.

"Of course I'm not okay, you moron."

She started to sob again, but clenched her fists to her side and swallowed the sob.

"I got to get out of here for a while."

Her voice was shaky as if she were struggling to make sure she didn't cry again, to try to get back some kind of control so she wouldn't have to show Bernie how dependent she was on him. He hated it when she did that. He wanted, just for once, for her to let herself go in front of him so he could take her in his arms and comfort her and tell her that everything was going to be okay, even if it wasn't, instead of putting up this angry show of strength to prove she could take care of herself, and didn't need or want his comfort, or anyone else's, for that matter.

The only time he had seen her fall apart was at the fire, but even then she didn't dissolve into sadness or sorrow or anything that could be comforted, but into rage, blistering, searing rage that had burned into his soul the way the fire had burned the backs of his hands.

"Your mother's driving me crazy," she continued. "She won't stop talking about it. And I can't talk about it anymore. I got to go somewhere for a while. Take me down to Axel's so I can get a beer and something to eat."

He told his father they were going down to Axel's and they'd be back in a couple of hours. His father nodded once, without taking his eyes off the television screen, and said, "Have a good time." His mother was still making whooping sounds in the bedroom, and it occurred to Bernie that if he were a stranger and didn't know that this was the way his mother cried, he would have thought she was going crazy.

4

Axel stood behind the bar polishing a beer glass when they walked in. He stopped what he was doing and stared at Bernie. Bernie knew that Axel was wondering what the hell they were doing here with their kids dead and all. Probably thought they should be home crying and carrying on. But Axel didn't know what it was like, didn't have the slightest idea.

"Hey, Ax," Bernie called. "How's it going?"

Axel nodded and arranged the glass on the bar next to the other clean ones, his eyes following as Bernie led Sarah to a booth. Bernie leaned over, asked Sarah if she wanted a beer. She said, "Yes."

"Two beers," Bernie said. "And a couple Slim Jims."

Axel dried his hands on a towel by the sink, picked up a glass, and held it under the beer spigot. He kept his eyes on the stream of beer as he spoke.

"Sorry to hear about the fire," he said.

"Yeah," said Bernie.

"You okay? Sarah okay?"

"We're just fine, Ax," said Bernie. "It's kind of tough, you know? But you've just got to hang in there."

"I guess that's true." Axel slid the two beers in front of Bernie. "Two bucks."

"Sarah'd like a sandwich. What kind of sandwiches you got?"

"The usual," said Axel. "Hamburgers, cheeseburgers, white hots, ham, ham and cheese, turkey. Think we got some beef tongue back there, too. Special."

"Make us a couple a ham and cheese. On white bread, with some mustard. We get pickles with that?"

"Sure do."

"Then let's have a couple a pickles with that, too."

Axel walked into the kitchen through the swinging door and came back out a second or two later.

"Sandwiches be out in a couple a minutes," he said.

Bernie took a sip of beer and started gnawing on the Slim Jim. Sarah sat across from him, looking down at the glass of beer and sniffling.

"You okay?" he said.

"Jesus Christ," she said and lifted her eyes from the glass. "Will you stop asking me that?"

She stood up and walked over to the jukebox in the corner. It was one of those old ones with flashing lights and lots of chrome and it still used those old 45s instead of CD disks. Sarah ran her finger along the selections, then popped a couple of coins into the slot, and punched some buttons. In about ten seconds, Loretta Lynn was wailing about something or other, Bernie didn't know what.

Sarah came back to the table, drained the beer from the glass, and turned toward her husband.

"Let's dance," she said.

"Dance?"

"Dance. Are you deaf as well as a moron?"

"No, I heard you. I just don't think we should, is all."

Sarah reached down and grabbed Bernie by the wrist, digging her nails in until he was almost ready to scream.

"Goddamn you, Bernie, you get up and dance with me right now or I'm gone to smack you right here in front of Axel and everybody else."

She kept hold of Bernie's wrist and led him to the dance floor. Axel watched the two of them from behind the bar, and every time Bernie looked his way, Axel lowered his eyes, pretending to concentrate on what he was doing.

The Loretta Lynn song ended, and another song started, something from the sixties: "When the night (bomp) has come (bomp bomp-bomp-bomp) and the land is dark..." Bernie started back to his seat, but Sarah held him. They continued to dance, not really moving very far, just swaying in place, and turning a little bit, slowly, like the second hand of a clock. Sarah closed her eyes and nuzzled her head into the hollow between his shoulder and neck, the way she used to when they were first going out years ago, the way he thought it should always be. She looked as if she were sleeping, her mouth slightly open, and it was only her shuddering every few moments that made him aware that she was fighting to hold back her tears.

He wanted to tell her he was sorry about everything that had happened. It wasn't as if he'd wanted the children to die. It wasn't as if he'd planned to spread lighter fluid all over the bottom of the stairs and toss the lighted match so that the fire would spread upward toward the children's room until, sound asleep and unaware of what would soon engulf them, Kimmy and Daniel burst into flames, their screams ringing through the house. That's not what he'd wanted at all.

He'd wanted to scare her, was all, wanted to let her know, Sarah, that she couldn't treat him that way, drinking every night 'til two or three hours past closing with her buddy, Gail, though he knew that her buddy Gail was really that Gary he had found her with a few weeks back.

He hadn't really thought much about it while he waited for her to come home, waited up through a couple of stupid movies on the comedy channel, and the more he waited, the more he worried, afraid that she might be dead somewhere, the car in flame all around her, or that she might be with that Gary or some other guy that she'd met in the bar. He pictured her in the alley out behind the bar, the guy clutching her head between his hands like a basketball or something, tight against his groin, and Bernie'd found himself filled with rage, hoping she would be dead because she'd promised she'd be back by midnight like she promised almost every night, and he'd believed her like he always believed her. Then she'd come stumbling into the house smelling like stale beer and Gary and said "Wha're you doing up?" and he'd mumbled something like, "I waited up for you," rubbing his hands back and forth on his pants legs, his fingers opening and closing, opening and closing, because what he really felt like doing when she said, "Asshole, whyn't you go to bed?" was to stab her with the knife he'd used to slice the ham for dinner tonight, because she'd done this to him a thousand times, but he couldn't because of the kids, because he knew what a horror it would be to have the kids come down in the morning and find their mother sitting against the refrigerator in a pool of blood. He couldn't do this to the kids. He couldn't do this to her. The kids really did love their mother, and she was a pretty good mother most of the time, even though she didn't wake up until after noon, which meant that he had to get up with them and feed them and play with them until she woke up and took over so he could go to work.

All he wanted was to scare her, show her he was important, too, that he could hurt her the way she'd hurt him, that he could hurt the kids if he wanted to, except that he didn't want to because they were his kids, too, and he loved them as much as she did, loved her, too, for that matter, so much that it felt like burning, except that everything had gone horribly, horribly wrong, not at all the way he thought it would, and he didn't know what to do about it.

After he lit the fire, he went outside to have a cigarette, pretending that he'd been outside all along, and stood by the old maple tree, watching the trucks go by on Route 7. She was supposed to run right up the stairs to get the kids as soon as she heard the smoke alarm, but he heard her yell, and when he looked back at the house, she was running toward him in that short little yellow nighty she had, asking him where the kids were.

The music stopped, and another song started.

Bernie turned to go back to the table, but Sarah pulled at him with both hands.

"Don't leave me, Bernie," she pleaded in a half whisper.

"But it's a fast one," he said. "It wouldn't look right."

"I got to keep dancing. If I don't, I'm gone to fall to pieces right here."

She held both of his hands and started to pump her legs up and down in a dancing motion. She forced a smile to her lips, though her eyes, still red from crying, were wild and desperate.

"Please," she said.

How could he say no? In spite of everything that had happened; in spite of the rage that still lay in ambush, knowing that she'd been seeing someone else and that she was only here with him because there was no one else to turn to, no one else who could love her as well as he could, and that he would lose her forever if he told her what he'd done; in spite of the sense that it was indecent to be dancing while Kimmy and Danny were lying in a plastic bag in the county morgue; in spite of all this, Bernie, because he never could deny her, danced.

Cleaning Up the Mess

Doris made all the arrangements. She's better at that sort of thing than I am. If it had been up to me, I would have just left it there. But she insisted the old barn's foundation was undamaged and we could build a new barn on top of it.

I didn't want anything to do with it. As far as I was concerned, all we really needed to do was clean up the mess so the kids wouldn't get hurt. We didn't need a barn, didn't own anything we needed to put into it, and couldn't afford to rebuild it. There were other things we could do with the insurance money—pay bills, put aside something in the savings for winter or to tide us over, since I was going to be out of work in a year and didn't know whether I'd be able to get another job, anyway. But Doris had other ideas.

Doris always has other ideas.

"I *need* to do this, Howard," she said. "You don't *know* how much that barn meant to me."

But I did know. The barn had meant as much to me as it had to her, though maybe in different ways. Doris called it her "Wyeth" barn, and invested it with attributes far beyond my comprehension. It made her happy the way candlelight made her happy, or a brick fireplace.

It had been built in 1876, and the man who built it—his name was French—had made the foundation, a ten-foot-high wall, from glacial rock he'd hauled in from his fields, rock deposited during the ice age millions of years ago when Lake Ontario still covered what is now the town of Sweden. Kevin, my eight-year-old, used to drag me out there to show me the new fossils he had discovered, mostly brachiopods smaller than my thumbnail, in a bit of rock that showed through the pink mortar that held everything together.

It was a beautiful barn.

One summer afternoon four years ago, right after my mother died, I climbed up to the second floor and stood by myself among the hay bales and smelled—no, watched—the sweetness of hay rise like incense toward the rafters two stories above my head. It reminded me of the cathedrals we had seen in England.

The day it burned down, all I could think was, "There goes my life up in smoke." A cliché, I know. But the cliché had become an image, and the image was real enough. A black column of smoke burst through the gambrel roof like a fist reaching to strike out the sun. The world turned dark, as if everything were coming to an end. Flaming shards of wood and shingle rained down over everything, and I brushed sparks from my hair and clothes and from the kids' hair and clothes. Firemen clambered over the house, soaking down the roof, the trees, whatever they could to make sure the fire wouldn't spread. But the barn was beyond hope.

When it was over, what was left stood like an elephant with its back broken. The roof had collapsed inward and fallen through most of the second floor to the horse stalls below. Now the whole structure, except for the stone foundation, was little more than a jumbled heap of scorched lumber that jutted up like splintered bones; soggy, half-burned hay; record albums melted together in blackened messes; the remains of a camper trailer Doris's brother-in-law had left for safekeeping; and a broken assortment of ax handles, spades, pitchforks, scythes, shears, picks, tackle, and saddles. Somehow the central beam that ran the length of the barn, though charred and probably useless, had remained intact and held up an unburned portion of the second floor.

I wanted to forget the whole thing. First the job, and now this. I didn't care anymore whether we had a barn or not. The house hadn't burned down, Doris and the boys were safe, and we hadn't lost anything we would miss anyway. *Sic transit gloria mundi.*

"A barn is good for the spirit," Doris argued.

So I relented, as I always do. As long as she made the arrangements, it was fine with me.

The real reason I let her make the arrangements was that I didn't like going through the trouble of getting estimates and dickering with contractors. Salesmen intimidate me. I'm the type of person who, if he wants to buy something, goes in and buys it without arguing about the price. If a salesman tells me, for instance, that a car costs $8,000, I'll pay $8,000, because I figure he knows what he's talking about. For Doris, on the other hand, the world operates like a Mexican street market.

"You've got to argue with these people," she insists. "They always ask for more than they'll take." So she argues, up one side and down the other. And she usually wins.

It was no trouble getting someone to rebuild the barn. Wayne Harris could do it for about $9500, and since he'd always done good work for us before, there was no good reason not to rebuild, Doris said, though it would not be as tall as the original—there would be no second story, only a roof on top of the foundation. All we had to do was haul away the charred wood and rubble and clear things up so he'd have room to work.

Doris talked to a half dozen people whose business it was to cart away wreckage, explained exactly what she wanted, had them put their estimates in writing. When she had all the information, we sat down to talk it over.

"Okay." She pulled out the first estimate and lit a Lark. "We can eliminate Ken Bidlack right away. He wanted to bulldoze the whole thing, wall included. When I told him he had to leave it standing because we wanted to build on top of it, he said he couldn't do it for less than $3,000. You agree?"

She sucked on the Lark and blew a cloud of smoke toward me.

"M-hm," I said. It didn't make sense to me to pay $3,000 to have someone carry off a load of trash, especially since we only had $10,000 from the insurance and Wayne would take all but five hundred of that.

"Fowler and Wright are out for the same reason. They're lower than Bidlack, but only by a hundred or two. The other contractors don't want to have anything to do with it. But I had another thought—stop chewing your beard—so I called Keith Wolanski and asked him, and he said if we could get some people to help, he could bring over his frontloader and his dump truck and do it for five hundred. What do you think?"

Keith Wolanski. A real Neanderthal. We had known Keith and his wife Karen for a few years because our kids went to school together. Karen was okay, a bright and warm-hearted person who devoted a lot of time to Scouts, the church, and to baking pies and cakes for various fund-raising projects. Keith was another story. He was a large man, completely bald except for the monkish fringe of hair around his head. A crease ran across the center of his face as if someone had once folded it over and forgotten to straighten it out.

In the time we had known him, I don't think he had ever spoken more than four words. His back yard had been taken over by a cement-mixing truck, a dump truck, a steamroller, a bulldozer, two frontloaders, and a backhoe. I still don't know what he did for a living, though I do know he made twice as much as I did teaching, but he spent his leisure time digging holes and pushing dirt around with the bulldozer. His life had been a direct progression from Tonka to Massey-Ferguson.

He liked to think he was pretty good at what he did, but the town of Sweden still remembered the time he broke open one of the town water lines as he was digging a ditch at the edge of his property.

"Well, he's not going to do any digging," Doris snapped when I reminded her. "And if it bothers you, you'll just have to keep an eye on him."

"Why should I have to keep an eye on him? You're the one who wants to hire him."

"You're the one who has the problem with him."

Wonderful, I thought. Keith and I have a great rapport. I talk and he grunts. I didn't say that to her, of course. Once Doris has her mind made up, there is no stopping her. Actually, I didn't say anything but, "Go ahead and call Keith, then."

She crushed the Lark in the ash tray and said, "What's really bothering you, Howard? Out with it."

"Nothing," I said.

"Don't tell me 'Nothing.'"

"It's nothing."

"All right." She lit another Lark. "Don't talk."

"I still don't think this is a very good idea."

"Oh, Howard, we've been through all this before. The insurance will cover the barn. And a year's a long time. Something will turn up. You'll see."

There was nothing more I could say. Once Doris proclaims everything is fine, there is no more talking to her. So I swallowed my reservations along with the sludge at the bottom of the coffee cup and said, "Do what you want."

Doris called about a dozen people and bribed them with a free lunch (which, of course, I would cook) if they would come over and load the barn onto Keith's dump truck.

Saturday morning around eight o'clock as I puttered around the kitchen—trying to convince myself not to go back to bed and pull the covers over my head, that everything was going to work itself out, that everything was going to be just fine, just fine—the dump truck lumbered into the driveway and back to the barn, the frontloader chained to its back.

"Doris!"

"What!"

"You'd better come down and take a look at this."

"What's the matter?"

She had come downstairs in a green bathrobe and pink, puffy slippers.

"Look at the truck."

"What's wrong with it?"

"No goddamn sides."

"So?"

"So? So how's he going to carry all that junk back to his place or wherever?"

She lit a Lark and blew out the smoke. "You worry too much, Howard."

"He'll be dumping shit all over the highway, for Chrissake."

"Listen, Howard." She turned away to pour herself some coffee. "It's not your problem. All you have to worry about is loading. Keith will take care of the rest. Have you started the spaghetti sauce? It has to be ready at noon."

She didn't wait for an answer and went upstairs to shower and dress. I finished my coffee and started the spaghetti sauce. Then I went out to the barn.

Flies plentiful as dust motes buzzed everywhere. The air stank of fermenting oats.

Keith's face was as red as a boiled beet from trying to start the frontloader. The machine whirred and whined but refused to start. Keith cursed, banged at it with a wrench, fiddled with some wires, tried to start it again, cursed and banged at it some more, but nothing happened. After more cursing and banging and fiddling with wires, the machine gave a farting sound followed by a bang, and roared into life. Keith jammed the gear shift into reverse, backed the frontloader down the truck ramp, spun it around, and raised and lowered the bucket a few times to make sure it worked.

"Listen, Keith," I said. "Watch out for the fence, and be careful of the wall. We want to rebuild the barn."

"Yup."

He tightened one of the hydraulic lines and climbed back onto the frontloader as if nothing else existed.

Up at the house a car door slammed. In another minute, Jim and Donna Damon and Steve Finch strolled toward the barn, ready to pitch in. Donna pecked me on the cheek and giggled "Hi Howie" at me. She had on work boots that looked as if they had never been worn, khaki work pants, and a matching shirt with creases so sharply pressed you could have sliced bread with them. Jim was wearing the same outfit and a shit-eating grin. What the well-dressed yuppie couple wears to clean up after a barn fire. They looked as if they had just stepped out of an L. L. Bean catalogue.

Steve, on the other hand, was dressed as if he had just returned from a four-week binge. He probably had. He had on a pair of baggy jeans frayed at the cuffs and torn at the knees, and a green sweatshirt that had been around since the signing of the Magna Carta. Toes poked up through holes in the tops of his sneakers. His blond hair stood in patches. He looked like a man on the verge of hysteria.

"Where should we start, How?" he said.

Before I could answer, there was a shriek of splitting wood. I turned just in time to see the frontloader jerk backward through the barn door, what was left of it. As Keith swung the frontloader around, the bucket, laden with rubble, missed the wall by less than half an inch.

"Jesus Christ, Keith. Watch out, will you?" I yelled.

The machine struggled toward me. I leaped out of the way. It continued through the opening in the fence, made a half turn left, stopped at the truck, raised the bucket high in the air, moved forward until the bucket was directly above the truck bed, then dropped the load. It backed away, wheeled in a half circle, and charged straight back to the burned-out barn.

I tried, without success, not to watch as he urged the frontloader in and out of the barn. At least a half dozen times he missed ramming the wall by a hair, and I prayed that when the day was over the wall would still be standing.

More people arrived: Dan and Alma Schaefer and their kids; Dave Tessy from Bio; Shelley Pangborn from Dance. When they were all assembled, Doris made her appearance. She was dressed in a pair of baggy overalls and one of my T-shirts and rushed forward as if she were very much harried. She herded all the children off to the front yard to play on the swings and assigned the rest of us an assortment of tasks.

Before long we were scurrying over the collapsed structure, dragging out what trash we could and arranging it on the back of the dump truck, each of us turning blacker and blacker by the minute, scraping our arms and banging our shins, the frontloader charging back and forth between the barn and the dump truck like some prognathous saurian. When the truck would hold no more, Keith tied down the load with a length of heavy chain and backed the truck out of the driveway. Scattering chunks of dirt, charred fragments of wood and roof tiles and rusty nails about Route 19, he carted the mess off and dumped it God knows where.

Later, when the truck came back, Steve started chatting about the situation at the college—what we called the "Monday Morning Massacre," thirty-seven tenured faculty eliminated in one stroke, me among them.

"Retrenchment," he said. "I love it. Don't you love it? It sounds as if we're waging war against something and losing. Five years. I give this place five years, then we'll all be selling pencils on the street corner. I've got it."

Together we lifted the charred beam and Steve started backing up the ramp to the truck bed.

"What are you bitching about, Steve? I'm the one who got the axe."

"Well, I…uh…know. But it's just…well, it's a damn shame. It's all Bob's fault. He could have…"

He was referring to Bob Wexler, our dean and former department chairman. I cut him off.

"Bob couldn't have done shit, Steve," I said. "It happened, that's all. Let's just forget it."

The beam dropped to the truck bed with a bang. Steve jumped back and nearly tumbled to the edge.

"Damn," he said, and pulled some slivers of wood from his hand.

Shortly before noon, Keith was ready to pull down the central beam. His idea was to hook one end of a chain around the beam and the upright supporting it, the other end of the chain around the bucket of the frontloader, and pull. My idea was that there was an easier and safer way of doing it, one that wouldn't risk pulling down the wall, too.

"You done this before?" he asked.

"Well, no."

"Then let me do what I'm being paid for. I ain't going to hurt your frigging wall."

I started to say something, but Doris stopped me.

"What's the trouble, Howard?"

"Look at this setup," I said. "He's going to pull the whole damn wall down that way."

"Howard, really. I think Keith knows what he's doing. Why don't you take a break and have a beer or something?"

"Stop trying to mollify me. I'm not a little boy."

"Go to hell, Howard," she said, and stormed away.

So we did it Keith's way. When he was ready, he climbed back up on the beast, jammed the gear shift into reverse, and let up on the clutch. The beast strained backward, the chain grew taut, the beams began to creak and groan, but nothing happened. Keith gave it more gas. The engine roared louder, the machine bucked like a horse with a burr under its saddle, but the wheels only dug deeper ruts into the dirt.

"Son of a bitch," said Keith, and kicked the tire.

"I told you it wouldn't work."

Keith glared at me and charged to the cab of his truck, took out a chain saw, and turned back toward me as if he had stepped out of a hack and splatter film. I backed out of his way as he pushed past and disappeared behind the wall. In a moment, the saw buzzed into life.

"Lunch, people," Doris announced.

Shelley Pangborn cornered me by the corral.

"You know, I'm terribly, terribly upset about what they've done to you."

"It wasn't personal, Shelley."

"I'm not certain about that. They could have taken Steven, you know. After all, he never even finished his Ph.D. Neither did Edgar Bailey, for that matter."

"Bad timing. That's all. They followed the terms of the contract—tenure date and all. I just happened to be the last one in the department tenured."

"That's an excuse. I think Wexler is still angry with you for opposing him on the Comm Skills program. He could have found a way to take Steven. Steven's a disaster in the classroom, Howard. Everybody knows it. Half the time he's not even sober. Do you know how many times he's been to the beer cooler this morning?"

I told her I hadn't noticed. She told me I should.

"Look, Shelley. I appreciate your concern, but right now I don't have time for this. I've got enough on my mind with this barn business."

"Sorry, Howard. I just wanted to let you know I cared."

We straggled back to the house, washed our hands at an outside water spigot, and gathered around the picnic table on the side porch because Doris didn't want us tracking soot and ashes all over the house. Before we sat down to eat, Doris grabbed me by the elbow.

"I want to talk to you, Howard."

She led me around to the back door by the dog pen.

"Now what's going on with you?"

"I don't know what you're talking about."

"You know damn well what I'm talking about."

"All I said was that his idea didn't work."

"Don't play dumb with me."

"Look, Doris," I said, throwing up my hands. "The man drives that thing around as if this were the Spenser Speedway. I don't know how many times he's just barely missed ramming into the doorway. And you just witnessed his latest effort to pull the whole goddamn thing down on top of himself."

"And I suppose you could do better, Mr. Smartass English Professor who can't hammer a nail through a board without hurting himself. When was the last time you drove a frontloader? Or did anything else around here, for that matter?"

"What is that supposed to mean?"

"It's that superior attitude of yours, Howard. I don't like it. You think you're better than he is just because you have a Ph.D.

Big deal. And you act as if he's responsible for everything that's happened to you."

"Come on, Doris. That's not it at all."

"It is so, and that's all it is. You know he doesn't have to do this, not for five hundred dollars, not at all. He's doing this because he likes us."

If anyone other than Doris had said this, I would have laughed. I couldn't imagine Keith liking anyone, or having any other kind of reaction toward anyone. Keith's reasons for helping, as far as I was concerned, for riding the beast's back and for pushing himself harder than the rest of us could push ourselves, was more basic than that, less complicated. He did it for the same reason that the beaver builds dams, or that the ant carries a hundred times its own weight, or that the African termite builds mud structures eight, ten, twenty feet high. It's what he did. He couldn't help it.

I didn't say this to Doris. She would have called me an intellectual snob.

As we ate, the chain saw stopped buzzing, and a few minutes later there was a large crash.

"Sounds like Keith got the beam down," said Steve. Dan Schaefer choked into his napkin. Donna giggled. Shelley Pangborn asked Dan to pass her some bread.

"I'll bet he did," I muttered.

"Aw, lighten up, Howard," said Dan.

"You're taking this too seriously," Dave Tessy chimed in.

"Things will turn out all right," Dan said.

"Sure," I said.

In a few more minutes, the truck creaked down the driveway and was gone. It was then that I noticed that, in addition to everything else, the truck had been tearing branches from the lilac trees that lined the drive. It was getting to be one damned thing after another.

Some time later when lunch was over, I went back out to the corral to find Keith gnawing on a sandwich. Something red and stringy dangled from it. He chewed on his sandwich and grunted at me as I walked by to inspect the latest of his handiwork.

Keith had managed to get the central beam down, all right, or at least part of it. But part of it still depended from a notch at the top of the stone foundation, and what he had brought down was a bigger pile of rubbish than we had already cleared away. There was no end to it.

I put on my work gloves and started hauling more stuff to the truck. Jim, Donna, Dan, Steve, and Dave were back at work a few minutes later. Doris and Shelley stayed behind to wash dishes and straighten up from lunch. Kevin and Mark played with the Schaefer kids in the front yard.

Keith finished his sandwich and climbed aboard the frontloader. Once again the beast roared into life.

For the remainder of the afternoon, I avoided Keith as much as possible. If I ignored him, let him do what he was going to do, maybe I could get through this without turning into Jack the Ripper.

And so it went, the beast scooping up its load of debris and dumping it on the truck, the rest of us hauling, lifting, and tossing, hauling, lifting, and tossing. There was soot and ashes all over our skin, in our hair, up our noses, in our lungs. The afternoon dragged itself along; our energy flagged. The creases had long since faded from the Damons' outfits, and Steve Finch looked positively haggard. Donna Damon was crying over her splitting nails.

But Keith was unstoppable. Though his T-shirt was sweat-soaked and his blackened face glistened like ebony, he kept moving. He was almost joyful. All I could think of was the African termite.

By four o'clock, we were nearly finished. What remained was that large section of the central beam that Keith had pulled down at lunch time.

Keith took out the chain again, wrapped one end around the bucket, the other twice around the beam, and hooked the ends of the chain together. With the chain extending from the beam at a forty-five degree angle, he climbed up on the frontloader and jammed it into reverse.

The beast groaned and strained, the wood snapped and popped, and as he gave it more gas, the engine roared louder and louder until I was sure it was going to blow up.

The engine hit its highest pitch, the chain snapped, whipped around and rattled against the bucket. The frontloader shuddered, lurched backward, Keith jamming on the brakes and trying to shove the gears into forward, and smacked against the stone wall. A diagonal crack appeared in the foundation, starting at the bottom corner of the doorway, and worked its way up like a river running upstream toward the top of the wall. I started to run.

Keith was moving his fingers along the edge of the crack, examining it as if he had just discovered stone. The tug in my chest had turned to nausea, and the nausea was turning to anger as I saw it was more than a hairline crack. He had moved a six-by-ten-foot section of the foundation six inches off its base.

"I can fix that easy," he said.

"You've already fixed it, asshole."

Doris grabbed my shoulder. "It can be fixed. He can push it back into place and Wayne will cement it back together."

I turned and glared at her. I wanted to hiss that it couldn't be fixed, could never be fixed, that nothing could ever be right again and that this cockamamie idea of rebuilding the barn was a pipe dream. But I didn't.

Instead, I turned on Keith.

"I don't want it back together. I want him out of here. Now. Before he wrecks everything."

"Howard, be reasonable." Doris stamped her foot at me. Water gathered at the corner of her eyes. They had all stopped and were looking at me, every one of them. Kevin and Mark stood with their eyes wide, watching daddy turn into a raving maniac.

"Reasonable?" I yelled. "What the hell is reasonable? Is any of this reasonable? All this jerk can do is knock things down with that stupid toy of his. This was a stupid idea, anyway. What the hell do we need with a barn?"

Keith didn't say a thing. He climbed up on the frontloader, no expression on his face, none at all. Slowly, deliberately, he put the frontloader in gear, raised the bucket, swung it around. It smacked into the top corner of the wall, and the wall, the goddamned wall, slowly, deliberately, crumbled to the ground.

Before I had absorbed what had happened, the frontloader growled past me and headed down the drive. Doris was red with fury, glaring at me—at me, not Keith. The rest—Steve Finch, Dave Tessy, Shelley Pangborn, all of them, the kids, too—so blackened with soot it was hard to tell one from another, stood motionless as if they had been encased in ice.

"Keith," I yelled. "Come back here."

But he didn't stop.

"Keith, you son of a bitch, what am I supposed to do about the wall?"

The frontloader turned onto Route 19 and kept on going.

"What am I supposed to do about the fucking wall?"

Behind me where the wall had fallen, the dust kept rising.

House in the Country

Larson found the house. He stumbled across it by accident one afternoon as he drove down one of those dirt roads people hardly traveled anymore. He stopped to pee and noticed what appeared to be another road, overgrown with weeds and bushes. And sure enough, it was another road. It was good enough to drive on as long as you didn't mind a few bumps, and as long as you stayed in second gear.

He followed the road for two and a half miles until there it was, a Victorian house, one with all sorts of gingerbread trim and curlicue designs along the eaves and soffits, and it was so far out of the way even vandals hadn't found it. There was only one broken window, and that on the second floor. A tree branch had apparently blown through during a windstorm. Some shingles had come off the roof—not many—most of the paint had peeled away, and some of the wood was rotting from the damp, but no human had done any damage to it.

The air was fresh, clean, and smelled of mint and wild thyme. Wisteria and wild grape grew over everything, including an old "For Sale" sign he uncovered. The sign was fading, but he could just about make out "Courtney Realtors" (he'd never heard of them), and "43 King Street" (he'd never heard of King Street, either).

It was the kind of place he had always dreamed of.

He could hardly wait to tell Moffitt.

It would be a good place to hide the girl.

They snatched her from in front of a neighbor's house as she was on her way home. It was one of those fancy neighborhoods where all the houses were designed to look Victorian or Edwardian. A sign on every street corner warned strangers that this was a "Neighborhood Watch" community, except no one was watching.

The little girl struggled at first, but eventually went limp and let them tie her up and tape her mouth. She hadn't made a sound. Didn't even scream when they grabbed her. Larson spoke gently to her, reassured her that they didn't want to hurt her, they only wanted money her father owed them. On the way to the house, she fell asleep.

They set her up in a little room on the second floor. On the outside wall was a rust-colored water stain that looked like a large, taloned bird. There was a bed with an old straw mattress, and they added a couple of army blankets in case it got cold at night. They nailed the one window shut and boarded it up from the outside to make sure she couldn't get away.

When they untied her and removed the tape from her mouth, she didn't say anything, didn't even look at them. There was no expression on her face, not anger, not terror, not anything.

They locked her in, and Moffitt stayed at the house while Larson went off to make the phone call.

It took him twenty minutes to drive to the nearest gas station. The telephone booth was by the road. It was one of the older ones, with the glass doors that slid shut and turned on a light when it closed. Names, telephone numbers, and obscene messages were scratched all over the walls and on the phone itself. He dropped in a quarter and punched in the number.

His stomach churned and his hand shook. He had never done anything like this before and wouldn't be doing it now if it hadn't been for the layoffs—the "downsizing," as they called it.

The day of the downsizing, two security officers had appeared at Larson's work location and told him his services were no longer required. They confiscated his tools, took his identification badge, and escorted him to the front gate, where they left him as if he were an ex-convict being released from a long prison term. He had stood there staring at the factory building, convinced there had been some horrible mistake, when a few minutes later two different security guards led his friend Moffitt to the front gate, each one holding an arm.

Tears had streamed down Moffitt's face, and he kept trying to tell them he'd been a good worker and this was all a big mistake. But the security people said they didn't know anything about that, they were just doing their jobs, and walked back toward the factory.

The number started to ring, then a recording clicked in: "The number you are calling is not in service. Please check your directory for the correct number. Thank you."

He pressed the coin release and retrieved the quarter from the chute. Then he thumbed through the phone directory, but couldn't find the number he wanted. He looked in the Yellow Pages for Bauer Electronics. There was no listing.

"What the hell," he muttered, and checked the cover of the directory to make sure he had the right town.

He put the quarter in the slot and pressed "0." When the operator answered, he said, "I'm trying to call Axel Bauer on 357 Spindrift Drive. Do you have a number for him?"

There was a brief silence. Then she said, "I have no such listing."

"How about a different address?"

"I have no Axel Bauer at any address."

"Any Bauer on Spindrift Drive?"

"No, sir."

"Is it possible that the number is unlisted?"

"I cannot give out that information, sir."

He asked her to check the number he had tried to call.

"There is no such number in service, sir."

He decided to try one more thing.

"Can you give me the number for Bauer Electronics, then?"

There was another brief pause, then, "I have no listing for Bauer Electronics."

"What do you mean, no Bauer Electronics?"

It was a trick. He was about to pursue the issue when it occurred to him that Bauer might have called the police already, and that they must have made some kind of arrangements with the phone company and were even now trying to trace the call.

He banged down the receiver and pushed the coin return lever. The quarter fell into the box.

How could the police have gotten involved so quickly? They'd only snatched the girl two hours ago, and Bauer couldn't even know that she had been kidnapped yet. Larson fished the piece of paper with Bauer's phone number out of his pocket and looked at it. He tried to remember where he had gotten the number. He didn't recall looking at a phone book, though he must have—didn't even remember writing it down.

When Larson arrived back at the house, Moffitt was sitting on the front porch. He stood as Larson climbed out of the car.

"Did you talk to him?"

"Phone was disconnected."

"Disconnected?" Moffitt looked as if he weren't quite sure what the word meant.

"Yeah."

"You mean with all that money he can't even pay his phone bill?"

"Jesus, I don't know. It was just disconnected, that's all."

"So what are we going to do now?"

"I don't know. Wait 'til tomorrow. Let him worry a bit. There's plenty of time. How's the girl?"

Moffitt didn't answer right away. He looked as if he had forgotten the girl, then remembered.

"I think there's something wrong with her. I brought her some food right after you left. She didn't touch it. Didn't even look at it or me. She just kept staring at that spot on the wall. She's spooky, Larson."

"Is she sick?"

"I don't know. I don't think so."

"We can't let her get sick."

The girl sat where they had left her on the edge of the bed. She hadn't moved. Her hands were folded in her lap and she stared at the water stain on the wall opposite. She didn't seem to be breathing. For a moment, Larson had the sensation that he was looking at a statue, or a stuffed doll. He placed his hand on her forehead. It was cool, but normal. There was a pulse.

He squatted down beside her.

"Margery," he said in a voice low enough not to frighten her. He tried to take her hand, but it wouldn't budge. She didn't resist him. He simply could not unfold her hands. He didn't force her to unfold her hands. He didn't want to hurt her.

He continued. "We're not going to hurt you. All we want is for your daddy to give us some money and then you can go home. I want you to give me his phone number so I can call him. Will you do that for me?"

She didn't answer. She didn't move. It was as if he hadn't spoken. She kept staring at the water stain.

"There's a nice sandwich here for you, peanut butter and jelly, I think. You'll feel better if you eat something."

Still no answer.

Larson looked up at Moffitt.

"See what I mean?" said Moffitt. "She doesn't move, doesn't do anything. She gives me the willies."

Larson stood. "She's upset, that's all. She'll get over it in her own time. We'll just let her alone until morning. Leave her sandwich and milk here in case she gets hungry."

But the following morning, the sandwich and milk remained untouched. The bed hadn't been slept in, and the girl hadn't changed her position. She hadn't even gone to the toilet. The chamber pot they had left in the room was empty.

Moffitt took the sandwich and milk down to the kitchen while Larson checked her forehead and pulse. They were still normal. She appeared healthy, but continued to stare at nothing.

When Larson walked into the kitchen, Moffitt said, "She's making herself sick, you know. She's trying to kill herself."

"Don't be stupid."

"She knows her father doesn't care about her, so she's just going to starve herself to death."

"She's scared, Moffitt. She'll get over it."

"You know what else?"

"What?"

"I've been listening to the radio all morning and I haven't heard anything."

"So?"

"So we grabbed her yesterday. That's plenty of time. There ought to be something."

"The police are keeping it quiet, trying to make us nervous so we'll do something stupid."

"Maybe we should let her go now before it's too late," said Moffitt.

"It's already too late," Larson said. "They'll still send us to jail if we get caught, no matter what."

Moffitt poured himself a cup of coffee and sat at the table next to Larson. "I guess you're right," he said. "What should we do now?"

"I don't know. I need a minute to think."

Larson realized that he hadn't planned this as well as he thought he had. After all, he wasn't a professional, had never kidnapped anyone before. If he had thought there was going to be even the slightest hitch, he never would have gone through with it. But he didn't say that to Moffitt.

Instead he said, "Okay, listen. Try to call Bauer again. If he doesn't answer, drive past his house, see if anything's going on. But don't do anything. Come back here and we'll figure out what to do."

After Moffitt left, Larson fiddled with the radio dial to see if he could get something besides the country and western station, but all he could get was static. Maybe it was the location. Or maybe the batteries were defective. He switched the radio off and decided to take a stroll outside. The girl wouldn't escape. Her door was locked and the window had been nailed shut.

The day was filled with sunshine and bird song. In a few minutes he had already seen cardinals, jays, and several finches. A solitary hawk circled overhead, gorgeous bird. The air was rich with the smells of mint and wild thyme. He was reminded of an earlier time when Amy, his wife, was still alive, before the cancer had taken her. This house was like the house they lived in before she died, the house he had tried to hold onto as long as he could, even after the layoff, but which he had to let go because you couldn't support a house like that on what they paid in unemployment checks.

Bauer Electronics had given the laid-off workers six months' pay and six months' medical benefits, and of course they could roll over their benefits into a retirement account or could take cash with a tax penalty.

That hadn't seemed a bad deal at the time, except that within a month after he was laid off, Amy had come down with the cancer. During a routine examination, the doctor found a couple of cysts on her ovaries that turned out to be malignant, and the two of them knew, without even saying it out loud, that this was the end, that she would be dead within six months, though the doctor did not admit it at first and tried to be optimistic about things.

Larson thought of it as "the cancer" rather than as the more generic "cancer" because it seemed to him a flesh and blood enemy, like "the executioner" or "the assassin," some physical entity dressed in a black hood with some kind of weapon in his hand that could only inflict pain and, ultimately, death.

The company's medical plan only covered half of the expenses for visits to the specialists, chemotherapy, medication, visits from the home nursing service. The rest he paid from the six months of salary until that ran out. Then during the last month of her life as he watched all the vitality drain from her, her color turn to gray, her flesh dwindle down to nothing until the skin draped across her brittle bones, translucent like silk or gossamer, he did what he could with the unemployment check, which wasn't very much.

By the time of the funeral, he was behind in his mortgage payments and having trouble with the car. He had to sell off the house, and by the time he paid all his bills, he had nothing left. Then he had taken a small apartment in a complex by the canal, but it was nothing like the house.

Nothing like this place either. Amy would have loved a place like this, so peaceful, so solitary. He wondered how it was possible for anyone to have abandoned—no, not abandoned, forgotten—this place. He felt he could stay here forever.

When he arrived back at the front door, totally relaxed and serene, he was surprised to find that two hours had passed. It was nearly noon. Moffitt should have been back some time ago.

At quarter to one the old Plymouth rumbled up the road and stopped in front of the house. Moffitt didn't get out. Larson went to the car to see what was going on and found Moffitt sitting in the front seat with his face in his hands. Larson called to him and Moffitt looked up. His face was pale, and for a moment Larson thought he had been crying. He stared at Larson as if Larson were a stranger.

"What's the matter?" Larson said.

Moffitt turned his face away as if he didn't dare to face Larson.

"I did what you told me. I tried to call Bauer. I got a recording. Said the phone was out of service. So I went to drive past Bauer's house." He stopped, looked around in the car as if he had dropped something.

"Well," said Larson. "Go on."

Again Moffitt turned toward Larson. Moffitt's face looked disjointed, as if it had been hastily pasted together by some lunatic artist. "I couldn't find it."

"Couldn't find it? How could you miss it? There aren't that many houses on Spindrift Drive."

"No. You don't understand. There's nothing there. There's no Spindrift Drive. I got to where it's supposed to be by the Stop-N-Go and there's nothing there, no street. I went around the block three times, and it still wasn't there. So I went in the Stop-N-Go and the kid said he never heard of Spindrift Drive. Said I must have the wrong name or the wrong town."

Moffitt stopped to catch his breath. His hands were shaking.

"Larson," he said, and his voice cracked. "What the hell is going on?"

Larson yanked the car door open. "Shove over," he said.

Moffitt slid over on the seat and Larson climbed in and started the car.

He should have known better than to send Moffitt on this errand, should have known that Moffitt would get nervous and begin to fall apart under pressure.

By the time they reached town, Moffitt had quieted down. He was still pale, and his eyes darted back and forth as if to make sure that everything was in its proper place, but he was no longer shaking, and his face was not quite so disjointed.

Larson waited at the Main Street intersection for the light to change. The BurgerMaster parking lot was full. The sign at the entrance proclaimed, "Over 14 billion served." He couldn't imagine fourteen billion hamburgers.

The light turned green. He turned two more blocks, and as he approached the Stop-N-Go, signaled for a right turn. He came abreast of the Stop-N-Go, but halfway into the turn, he put on the brakes. Moffitt was right.

There was no street.

There was a parking lot, and beyond that, fields and hedgerows. But no street.

Larson pulled into the parking lot and switched off the ignition. He could feel Moffitt looking at him, but he didn't look back. If he looked back, the panic he had seen earlier in Moffitt's eyes would leap out and seize him, and he was convinced there was some rational explanation.

He climbed out of the car without saying anything to Moffitt and went into the Stop-N-Go. A college boy sat on a stool behind the counter looking at a *Playboy*. He put the magazine under the counter and pretended to arrange the cigarettes. Larson walked to the back of the store and picked up the phone book. There was no Axel Bauer or Bauer Electronics listed.

He walked back to the front of the store and decided to take a chance that there had been no news of the kidnapping.

"Pardon me," he said to the boy. "Do you know if someone named Axel Bauer lives around here?"

The boy shook his head. "Never heard of him."

"You know. The head of Bauer Electronics?"

"Never heard of it."

Larson chuckled. "How is that possible? Half the town's employed by Bauer Electronics."

The boy pushed the hair back from his eyes and grinned. "I get it. You're from the television, right? Trying to play a trick on me to see how I react, right?"

"What gave you that idea?"

"Easy. I lived here all my life and there's no Bauer Electronics."

Larson's first impulse was to call the boy a liar, but if he did that, he'd call too much attention to himself.

Instead he said, "You're a pretty bright kid. We'll be in touch."

He went back outside and stood at the car for several minutes studying the area. Moffitt hadn't moved. Everything seemed normal, everything seemed to be where it should be—the Stop-N-Go, the car wash across the road, the motel the next block down—everything but Spindrift Drive.

Something turned over in Larson's stomach and began to crawl toward his chest: the panic he had seen in Moffitt's eyes. He began to get that unpleasant sensation of vertigo you get when you first look into a set of facing mirrors and see an infinity of mirrors, or when you see something out of the corner of your eye, only to turn your head and find it gone.

He made a mental inventory of everything. Margery Bauer, five years old. Axel Bauer, founder and CEO of Bauer Electronics. Residence, 357 Spindrift Drive. Bauer was worth millions. Bauer Electronics had recently laid off 100 workers, including Larson and Moffitt.

There was no Axel Bauer listed in the telephone directory. No Bauer Electronics listed. There was no Spindrift Drive. There was only a little girl who sat stone still on the edge of a bed in an abandoned house they had found, and who stared at a water stain on the wall.

Larson eased out of the parking lot and headed back the way he had come. At the intersection, he stopped for a light. His gaze fell on the street sign and the hair on the back of his neck bristled. Moffitt was weeping softly beside him. In another moment he was aware that the car behind him was beeping. The light had turned green.

He turned left, cutting off a blue Volkswagen coming in the opposite direction.

King Street was an old street, lined on both sides with seedy shops that looked as if they were barely surviving. There was a tailor shop, a shoe repair shop, a bicycle shop, a bakery or two, several greengrocers, and a butcher shop. Children played in the street, and three teenage boys loitered outside a soda shop.

It was odd that he hadn't noticed this street before. No. The street hadn't been here before. Spindrift Drive had been here before, but wasn't here now. His mind raced through the possibilities, but only one was logical, only one didn't sound like the plot of a bad science fiction story. Something had affected his brain. Some tumor had rearranged his neural passages, rewired the synapses so he remembered things that had never happened and relocated things that had.

As the numbers went lower, he slowed down, and when he came to 43, he pulled up to the curb and stopped. Forty-three was abandoned. The door was boarded up and bolted with an iron bar and a double padlock. Metal grating covered the window so vandals couldn't put rocks through it, but "Courtney Realtors" was stenciled on the window in gold, though the stenciling had faded. A single sign in the left hand corner of the window was also faded by sunlight and time. The sign read, "FOR SALE! Enquire within."

Below the words was a photo of the same abandoned house Larson had found in the country.

He caught his breath and bent to examine the photo more closely. There was no wisteria and no wild grape and no broken window and no shingles torn off the roof, but the same gingerbread trim and curlicue designs adorned the eaves and soffits. It was the same house.

Larson pressed his face as close to the window as he could and shaded his eyes to see inside. The windows were grimy. Inside the store there was nothing, not a desk, not a waste basket, not a chair. Nothing but dust. On the walls were vague outlines of what might have been picture frames and filing cabinets. Toward the back of the store was an open door through which Larson could see nothing but darkness.

A hand fell upon his shoulder and he spun around.

He found himself facing a policeman. The policeman was young, almost a teenager, with a slim face and a large gold moustache.

The policeman said, "Sorry, sir. I didn't mean to startle you."

"That's all right, officer."

"Something I can help you with?"

"No. Just curious about this place."

"Courtney's? This place has been empty since old man Courtney died, fifteen, twenty years ago."

"Do you know anything about this house?" Larson gestured at the photo in the window.

The policeman looked at the photo a moment, then shook his head. "Can't say that I do. Doesn't look familiar to me. Probably torn down a long time ago."

"Thanks for your help, officer."

"Anytime."

Larson climbed back into the car and started the engine. He continued down King Street. He wanted to see what it looked like. When it ended, it turned into a country road, and before long he found himself driving past farmland where everything looked familiar and unfamiliar at the same time. He passed a field of cows chewing on the grass. One of them looked up at him. He passed a barn with an ad for Red Man chewing tobacco painted on the end of it. The barn was familiar, but there was something not quite right about it. Maybe it was on the wrong side of the road, or set at a slightly different angle than he remembered. Or maybe the ad was at the wrong end. He couldn't figure it out.

As he was about to turn around and retrace the route they had taken, he came to the dirt road. He was surprised to find that he was approaching it from a different direction. He turned into it and shifted down to second gear.

Moffitt put his hand on Larson's arm.

"Where are we going?"

"Back to the house."

"I don't want to go back. I can't go back. We can't go back." Moffitt spoke as if the words were being squeezed from him.

"Don't be stupid."

"Can't you see? Everything's changing. Everything's falling away. It's like being inside a mirror. If we go back, something's going to happen."

"Easy, Moffitt." Larson spoke slowly, measured his words carefully so as to reassure his friend. "Someone slipped us something. It affected our minds so we can't remember right. We'll go to a doctor. He'll help us, give us something. That's all it is."

Moffitt pulled on Larson's arm. Larson slammed on the brake and the car stopped.

"It's not us," cried Moffitt. "It's outside us. It's something else. I don't know what."

Larson grabbed Moffitt by the shirt collar and shook him.

"Now you listen to me. It's nothing. Nothing's going to happen at the house. We've got to go back and get the kid, turn her loose. We can't leave her there alone."

"Kid?"

"Margery Bauer."

"WHO THE HELL IS MARGERY BAUER?"

Larson shoved Moffitt back against the seat, and Moffitt began to whimper. Larson ignored him and drove on. In a few more minutes they were pulling up to the house. Larson got out. Moffitt stayed in the car. The afternoon was still bright and glorious. High in a tree, a cardinal went "chick-chick." A hummingbird flitted past Larson's face. A hawk circled overhead.

Larson climbed the porch steps and pushed the door open. He turned to say something to Moffitt.

The car was gone.

He listened for the sound of the engine, and heard nothing but the call of birds. He jumped from the porch and ran down the road. Moffitt couldn't get far very quickly. Larson should be able to catch up with him running. He tripped on a wild grape vine and went sprawling, but picked himself up immediately. He kept running. He should catch up with Moffitt any minute.

He turned a bend in the road.

And found himself running up the drive toward the house.

The breath rasped in his lungs. The sweat on his back seemed to freeze. He must have hit his head when he tripped and become disoriented.

He turned and ran back down the road. This time he leaped over the grape vine, and when he came to the bend in the road, found himself back at the house.

It was pointless to turn around. There was nothing else to do but go in the house.

He walked through the front door, climbed the stairs to the second floor, and walked down the corridor toward the room the child was in. He removed the key from his pocket, placed it in the lock, and turned it until the bolt clicked back. He pushed the door open and stepped into the center of the room. Except for a single bed pushed against the wall, the room was empty. Margery Bauer was gone.

Larson corrected himself. Margery Bauer had never been there. Margery Bauer didn't exist, had never existed. He turned back to find the door closed behind him.

He hadn't heard it close.

He reached for the handle and turned it. It was locked, and he'd left the key in the lock on the outside. He kneeled and looked through the keyhole. There was no key. No way out. The door was locked. The window was nailed shut and boarded up.

Larson sat on the edge of the bed and stared at the water stain on the wall, the talons growing larger, closer. He was totally peaceful. Totally serene. The air was rich with the odors of mint and wild thyme. He felt he could stay here forever.

The Temptations of Guthlac

Two guardians keep watch about me: one dark as night, dark as the abyss that beckons, dark as my own soul; the other a creature of light, brighter than the sun, his aspect so dazzling I cannot look upon his face.

The two contend for my soul.

At night, the dark one speaks: "Strive for this world, friend Guthlac. Take joy only in what your hands can touch, your tongue can taste."

There is much to be said for his advice, and he tells such wonderful tales. His best begins, "Hear! We have heard the glory of the Spear-Danes..." I can almost see the bone-crusher gliding from the moors, Hart Hall sinking into desolation. At times he conjures marvels to please my sight: rocks dance to the sound of his voice, apples appear from nowhere, then vanish once again. He spreads a table before me laden with bread, cheese, wine, spices from the Orient.

"A riddle," he says. "I come where many wise men sit at council. I have one eye, two ears, two feet, twelve hundred heads, two hands, arms, and shoulders, one neck and two sides. What is my name?"

"I don't know," I say.

"Take a guess."

I scratch my head. Twelve hundred heads?

"I give up."

"A one-eyed garlic seller, of course," he answers, and pulls a rabbit from the air.

The bright one, though I cannot see his face, disapproves but says nothing. He stands still and rigid as a stone cross. These fifteen years he has said only two things: "This life is fleeting joy," and "You have the power to choose."

For years I have prayed for a sign of God's favor: a burning bush, perhaps; water from a rock; to be lifted up in a whirlwind. Instead, the guardians appeared.

It is all so very confusing.

Sometimes the dark one is gone for days, even weeks, and I am left with the greyness of the fens. To amuse myself, I turn to the bright one.

"Are you an emissary of the Lord?"

Silence.

"Did the Lord send you to aid me?"

"You have the power to choose," he replies.

"What kind of answer is that?"

Again, silence.

"Does God even exist?"

"You have the power to choose."

"But…but…how can I know which choice is right?"

"This life is fleeting joy."

"Pah." I spit and return to my barrow.

Three days have passed since the dark one vanished this time. The bright one has neither moved nor spoken. He merely stands, passive as a candle. For three days the sky has remained grey, the air grows chill. Winter will soon be upon me.

My neighbors have become restless of late. They do not appreciate my presence here. Though the fens are not much good for anything, the natives hereabout feel I have displaced them. Some are peasants who claim the fens for their own since the bretwald will have nothing to do with them. They are suspicious of outsiders, and I am sure they suspect my aristocratic birth and fear that my presence is some sly attempt of the king to reclaim the fens. Others simply distrust the clergy. The remainder are thieves, highwaymen, and murderers who have sought the fens as a refuge from the king's justice. They lurk about at night, self-exiled.

They have not attacked me.

Yet.

But that will come.

I believe they have designs on my barrow, though I can't imagine why. There is nothing here but me. When I first came, it was clear the place had been ransacked, body and booty, as have all the burial mounds scattered about. Thieves were not the only ones to plunder these ancient graves, vestiges of some druidical sect that spoke with the dead and summoned demons, I imagine. It has been reported, perhaps with some justification, that the king himself broke into one of these barrows and carried off great hoards of gold and jewelry to distribute among his retainers. Another rumor is that the noble abbot Redwald dug up one of these graves to support our monastery at Repton.

A blasphemous lie.

On the other hand, there would have been no sacrilege since this was, 'til I came, heathen ground.

In any event, this morning a shaggy man appeared across the fen to watch my island barrow.

"Praise God!" I called to him.

He did not answer.

"Sing glory to the Lord!" I called again.

He stood unmoved.

For the better part of the morning, he studied my every action until I began to wonder: could there still be treasure buried in my barrow? I crawled into the barrow and dug. There was nothing there.

"This life is fleeting joy," said the bright one.

This evening, things take a rather grim turn. A troop of shaggy men bearing torches, their faces lit like fiends', gathers in the fens.

"Guthlac," they jeer. "War-player."

Oh, to be born with such a name. They remind me of my career as warrior—something I had forgotten, or at least have been trying to forget—of the years I had spent hacking men to pieces with my sword, until the sight of one severed head, blood clotting its beard, swollen tongue protruding, brought me to my senses. I seemed to see my own head, to face my own end. This is what it meant to be a warrior. The sound of my true name brings back visions of that head, and I shudder.

The troop of shaggy men hoots across the fens. They accuse me of causing all their suffering, of displacing them from their rightful abodes. They threaten to repay me for my crimes: my flesh will feel the dread surge of fire (there is at least one poet among them), flames will devour my body. Arms and legs will be torn from me, my head will be paraded on a pointed stick. Their hounds will gnaw my bowels.

Rocks the size of a man's fist fly across the fens. Most of them splash harmlessly in the water just short of the barrow, but one strikes my left shoulder, and I cry out in pain. The clamor grows.

Another stone glances off the top of my head. I spin around toward the guardian, but quickly turn away, the brightness of his face nearly blinding me.

"Do something before they kill me," I plead.

The bright one does not move.

"Please." Another rock strikes my back.

"This life is fleeting joy," he says.

"Shit," I say, and turn back toward my barrow.

Their chanting increases. They curse God, His angels, and all His saints; they curse Satan and his demons. They yell out all manners of blasphemies and obscenities.

"We're gonna roast your bleedin' arse, Guthlac," shouts one.

"'Ey Guflac. Yer muvver's diddlin' the abbot," screeches another.

I hear myself accused of self-abuse, fornication, adultery, incest, sodomy, pedophilia, necrophilia, bestiality, and numerous other perversions for which there are no names. They challenge my parentage, my honesty, my courage, my devotion.

I pray for the dark one to return. Surely he can do something to save me. Perhaps some of his fancy juggling would distract them. Or one of his tales. Or he could turn them into toads or trees or rocks.

But he does not come.

I am alone.

Perhaps I should quit this place and return to Repton. The brethren would welcome me back, would not chide me for my weakness, indeed, would honor me for my perseverance. After all, I have endured this place for fifteen years. And the monastery walls would protect me from those who want to roast my "bleedin' arse."

It is not pride that has kept me here. It is not faith, either. The bright one has seen to that. It is difficult to believe in something that does nothing. Perhaps he is, as I've always suspected, a metaphor my mind has projected into visible form and over which I have lost control. It did not matter as long as the dark one was here, he, too, a metaphor, to keep the other in balance, the one to tempt me, the other to give me hope. But with the dark one gone, the bright one is useless. He gives no comfort, does not protect me from my enemies, and is no proof against the chill of winter.

It comes to this: if the bright one is real, God's messenger, I must endure my trials or I am damned. If he is not real, then the dark one, who also cannot be real (like God, a metaphor), is correct: it is more logical to heed the shaggy men and leave this place, to join the thieves and highwaymen, to follow the natural inclinations of the flesh, to rape, pillage, and burn, than to deny myself as I have for fifteen years.

Am I willing to take that chance, to leap into the void, to abandon all hope of salvation?

Yet the bright one shines.

I have not the courage to make *that* choice.

I pray that the shaggy men will leave me in peace.

A screaming comes across the sky and I lift my head. They come on rafts lashed together with rope and vines. The bright one does not move a thumb's breadth, but keeps repeating, "This life is fleeting joy. This life is fleeting joy," 'til I think I will go mad.

They charge right through him, clubs and knives raised, teeth bared, hungry for my blood.

How do I survive? Some will tell you that the Hand of God appears, as it was said to have appeared at my birth, to cast them off. None of it is true.

I struggle like a wild beast when the first blow falls, striking out at them with every bit of strength at my command. I have no wish to die. I kick, punch, bellow, sink my teeth into them.

Suddenly, only one of them remains, a sturdy brute, his face scarred and ugly with a nose like a toad, his chest as large as a hogshead. He smells of sheep shit, an odor so overpowering, I begin to retch. He seizes me by the throat, ready to plunge his knife into my face. I thrust my knee into his groin as hard as I can. He groans, drops the knife, rolls away, but does not let go. We tumble over and over and come to rest, he astride my chest, squeezing at my throat until I feel my eyes bulge out.

My hand claws the ground, and like a miracle, it is there, a rock the size of a melon. The voice of the bright one floats toward me: "You have the power to choose."

I choose.

I bash his fucking head in.

There is a soft, wet thud. The hands loosen from my throat, and he collapses on top of me like a sack of grain.

For several minutes I lie breathless with my eyes closed, his weight pressing me into the dirt, and I pray, over and over: "…sed libera nos a malo."

When I regain my breath, I push the body from me, sit up, and look around. The rest of the shaggy men are gone, vanished as if they had never been there, like the dark one's apples. All that remains is that solitary corpse. Brains leak from his shattered skull. Blood streams across his eyes and nose and into his gaping mouth. Bits of brain and gore cling to the rock in my hand. My rags are spattered with his blood, my hands wet and sticky.

I have not killed a man in years, had vowed never to kill again. How easy to break one's vows.

I dip my thumb in his blood and make the sign of the cross on what remains of his skull.

"Lord, let not thy vengeance fall heavy on the head of thy servant…"

Then I crawl into my barrow and claw out handful after handful of dirt. By dawn I have dug a hole three feet deep. Very carefully, I roll the body into the grave and cover it over with dirt and leaves. His grave is now the bed on which I sleep.

The shaggy men seem to have lost interest in me. They have not attacked again, have not even appeared. I find myself lapsing into boredom once more. I perform my daily tasks: gather roots and berries, collect firewood against the coming season. I remain dutiful in my devotions. I continue to chant my psalms, recite the canonical hours with all the fervor I can muster. What else can I do?

The bright one has not spoken since the night of the attack. His silence is a rebuke.

"It's not my fault," I cry. "The rock came into my hand." And it is true. The bright one had tricked me, had placed the rock into my hand and said that I must choose, knowing full well there was only one real choice. He has turned me into a murderer once again.

It has rained, a chilling rain that pierces the skin like hot cinders. It has been a struggle to keep my modest fire going, so I spend my time huddled inside my barrow, out of the wind, atop the dead man. This morning, ice glazes everything: the limbs of trees, the rocks, the very ground itself. Mist rises from the fens like the spirits of the dead.

A small voice sings out my name.

"Father Guthlac. Father Guthlac."

A young girl glides through the mist, poling her way across the water on a small raft. She is dressed in rags, her skin blue with cold. I judge her to be about fourteen.

The raft bumps against my little island, and she jumps ashore to stand shivering before me.

"Come, child," I say. "Warm yourself by the fire."

She does not speak, but kneels and rubs her hands slowly over the flame. She drinks the sage tea I make for her until the blue has gone from her face.

"Why do you come here?" I ask.

"My father sent me." She blushes and lowers her eyes.

Her name is Eadwig, and a pretty thing she is, though her hands are rough from labor and chapped from the cold winds. Her father, a peasant, has sent her to beseech me to leave this place.

"I have an oath, child. To leave would be an offense to God Almighty."

"But they will kill you," she says, regarding me with sadness, her eyes as blue and innocent as ice.

Before I can move to stop her, she loosens her rags and stands naked before me.

"We cannot let them kill you," she says.

I am trembling, but not from cold. Her skin is pink and fair in the firelight, her breasts perfect globes of spring fruit. She takes my hand and kisses it, the tip of her tongue darting against the hollow of my palm. The barrow becomes exceedingly warm. I feel the hardening in my groin, and wish for all the world to leap up and ravish her this very instant. I touch her cheek, soft as a coney's pelt.

"Behold, thou art fair, my child," I murmur, voice dry and cracking. I yearn toward her, raise my arms to enfold her, and hesitate.

My arms drop to my sides, and I speak again.

"Child, must you do this?"

Eadwig blinks her eyes, puzzled.

"You do not want me?" she says.

"Do you not understand that you are a temple for the Lord?"

"But I know I can please you," she says, reaching for my groin.

"Go," I say, handing back her rags and averting my eyes. "Tell your father I must stay."

"But he'll beat me," she cries, half in anger, half in terror.

"Then go elsewhere. You must not remain here. Do not give yourself to the wickedness of the flesh. Store up your treasures in heaven. This life is fleeting joy."

My own words amaze me, but I am terrified that my loins will betray me and that I will fall upon her like some beast of the field. I must say something to drive her from my sanctuary before I am lost, before she is lost.

She dresses, glaring at me as if I am a madman, then scurries out of the barrow.

When the raft has vanished in the mist, I strip naked and scourge myself with a hazel branch until my back is bloody.

I cannot sleep. The dead man beneath me troubles my dreams. He beckons, brains leaking from the hole in his skull, and I am bathed in blood. I try to run, but my feet stand fast. He embraces me until our faces touch, his nose against my nose, my eyes drawn into the scarlet void behind his eyes. My own screams awaken me.

I sleep again. Eadwig appears, naked and fair, her lips blood red. I, too, am naked. Her arms snake around my neck, my flesh presses against her flesh, and I feel myself weakening, sinking, as if the fen itself has come alive and is dragging me under. I am beside myself with passion, and I wish to have done with the struggle, to be at rest, at zero, to not have to strive among the contradictions: the palpable insistence of the flesh, the vague promptings of the spirit. But my member finds no entrance. She laughs at my impotence. I awake to dampness freezing in my groin.

A groan escapes me as I lie once more among dead leaves and twigs. A chill wind blows into my barrow, carrying with it darts of sleet. I huddle beneath my rags and fancy the dead man stirring beneath me.

The bright one stands outside, silent and resolute as ever, his face adazzle.

I must pray. When one founders, one must find some rock to cling to.

I kneel atop the dead man's breast.

"Oh Lord, make haste to help me."

Scarcely have the words passed my lips when the barrow fills with foul spirits. From all sides they swarm. They creep up through the floor, down through the roof. Nothing will keep them out.

Some are no larger than my hand, with forked tails, pinched faces, dripping mandibles. Others are as large as whales. They have heads like monkeys, boars, wolves, and lizards. Some have arms that writhe serpent-headed. Flames vomit from their throats, blood dribbles from their jaws. And from all their gaping mouths comes a strident caterwauling that swells until heaven and earth are filled with their bellowing.

Before I can take a breath, they seize me by the ankles and drag me toward the murky fen. Thorn bushes lacerate my flesh, my head thwacks against a rock. I cry out to the bright one, "Help me."

He stands unmoved.

They beat me with whips, with hazel branches; they touch burning coals to the soles of my feet, and yank tufts of hair from my head and beard. Then they lift me once again and bear me aloft, with a frightful whirring of wings, to the icy reaches of the sky. There they are joined by a legion of demons, leather-winged, rodent-faced, who wheel in flight and sweep me off to the jaws of hell itself.

My stomach heaves toward my throat, and I vomit gouts of root, bile, and finally air. Below, the seething cavern of fire, shaped like a dragon's jaws, roars at me. Flames belch from topless mountains, funnels of sulfurous liquid lurch toward me. Here and there among fire-blackened pits and burning pools scurry vaguely human figures, heads where their groins should be, arms growing from their rumps, mouths screaming from their bellies.

I shudder in fear.

The voices of the demons echo in my ears.

"We own the power to cast you into these depths. Here is the fire, enkindled by your sins. See how the gates gape open to receive you. See how the bowels of Styx churn to devour you."

My own bowels loosen in terror. The odor of my own excrement fills my nostrils. I wrestle to maintain my courage, to keep myself from being cast into the pit. I cry out with false bravado:

"W-w-woe to you, s-s-sons of darkness. You are b-b-but dying cinders among the ashes, images my diseased brain has fashioned. I c-c-care nothing for you."

They let me drop.

I plummet from the sky, their laughter filling my ears. The pit rushes toward me, swirling, teeming, seething, changing shape. It becomes the face of the man I had decapitated fifteen years ago, the face of the shaggy man whose brains I had dashed in. It becomes my own blood-drenched face, mouth gaping wide to swallow me.

I plunge into the darkness.

I awake on the frozen ground beside my barrow, the bright one silent above me. Perhaps this has been another of my hideous dreams. But I feel the welts from the whipping, the blisters on the bottoms of my poor, scorched feet (I can barely stand), the scabs on my head and face where they pulled out my hair. I curse them, every one.

I curse God, too. I had cried out to Him for help, and what does he send? A horde of demons.

I have had enough of gods and demons.

I crawl back into my barrow and try to start a fire.

I grow ill. My wounds fester and I am feverish. I cough, I sneeze, and at night I am shaken by spasms. I gather roots, and wood for the fire, try to keep myself warm, apply poultices to my wounds, place cold compresses to my head to subdue the fever. But nothing works. Day by day the disease worsens. Fever consumes me, and I am fettered from within. More pain comes to me now than on the night the fiends tormented me.

The bright one mocks me with his silence. A strange light shines from him as if my illness pleases him. He wishes me to see my affliction as a sign of God's grace, but I will not fall for that. I have nothing more to say to him, not even to curse him.

If the abbot were here now, what would I tell him? That the world is insanity, that faith is insanity, that anyone who would willingly forsake the comforts of kith and kin to live in the woods on roots and berries and suffer such travail is a lunatic? That it makes more sense to kill yourself?

He would not believe me.

And it is not for me to shatter his illusions, to crack his faith. No. So I would tell him lies, grandiose lies, lies so outrageous that the truth would shine forth in all its dark glory: "This life is fleeting joy, given to pain and sorrow. Seekers of pleasure shall know the grim guesthall, deep under the earth, where fire and the worm endure forever. Lay up your treasures in heaven. Trust only in the God of Abraham. He alone judges true. To heaven will he lead the souls of the faithful where are light and life and eternal bliss."

Winter passes. Spring arrives. Gillyflowers bloom everywhere. Birds twitter in the branches of trees, the sound drifting in like flakes of snow. A sparrow settles at my feet, cheeps, cocks his head, shits, and flits away.

I grow weaker, some days scarcely able to gather enough wood to keep the fire going during the cool nights. Pus runs like chrism from my wounds. How much longer can I endure? I would like to pray, try to pray: "Lord…have…mercy." The words are ashes, leave the taste of bile.

Easter morn, the day of Resurrection. My death day. My bones cry out the message. Soon this temple of flesh shall become one with the grave, this barrow I have made my home, limbs stretched upon the clay.

It is a struggle to raise my head, to lift myself up, but I make the effort to survey what is left of me: flesh overgrown with scabs and sores, bones nearly visible. I have become a living chancre. I fall back, exhausted. The corpse beneath me stirs, eager for a companion.

Suddenly, the dark one is there, as genial as ever, tossing a golden ball in his hand. The bright one is silent.

"Ah, friend Guthlac. You really have gone to seed. You see what happens when I'm not around? Everything falls apart."

He throws the ball into the air. The ball divides, becomes three, then six, then nine whirling 'round and 'round.

"No matter," he continues. "Tell me, did you enjoy the show? The shaggy men? Eadwig? The visit to hell? Oh, you were not pleased. At least it kept you going, gave you the opportunity to struggle. I've always admired that about you, Guthlac, your ability to struggle. It is your most endearing quality."

His hands weave a dizzying pattern to keep the balls in motion.

"But don't lose heart. It has all been worthwhile. Let me tell you what will happen. You will be buried with all the pomp and ceremony of the church."

The balls revolve in intricate circles around the golden ball.

"You will be sainted. An abbey will be erected in your honor on this very site."

One ball leaps from its orbit and he catches it behind his back.

"A few years hence, a monk named Felix, a man of great learning and imagination—too much imagination, some would say—will render an account of your life."

He reverses the direction of the spheres.

"A few years more, and a heroic poem will be composed in your praise: 'Now must we name what the Lord made known, how Guthlac kept his heart in God's favor, forsook the world's glory to seek his home in heaven.'"

He reverses direction again.

"Yes, Guthlac. Your name shall live beyond you from generation to generation,"…the spheres wink out…"even"…one…"to the end"…by…"of time"…one.

The air is empty, the spheres vanished.

The mockery, the arrogance. Have I gone through all this, suffered such indignities, had my flesh rent, torn, and scored to become a character in another of his stupid poems?

"You are upset, friend Guthlac. Please don't be. It was nothing personal. It's all metaphor anyway."

He stretches his hand toward me, beckoning.

This is an outrage. I would rip his throat out, deny him, dash his brains in had I the strength. I try to raise myself, but the effort is too much and I collapse on dead leaves.

Suddenly, the bright one slides forward and fills the barrow with light. They seize each other by the throat, each intent on the other's destruction, and the air is filled with their cries. The sun winks out, the sky takes on a purplish hue, the moon fades to the grey of rock. Huge clumps of earth pelt me from the roof of this barrow until I believe I will be buried alive.

They swirl around me. Light absorbs darkness, darkness absorbs light. Slowly, inexorably, I am drawn into the vortex of their struggle until they surround me completely.

"You have the power to choose," intones the bright one.

"You have the power to choose," mocks the dark one.

Light and dark enfold me, consume me, weave their way in and out of me, my eyes, my ears, my nostrils, my mouth. I clutch at leaves and cry out in anguish:

"What are these guardians? Who are they? Where do they come from? What do they want of me?

"My God, what are these metaphors by which I live?"

The Art of Courtly Loving

The minute Arthur Clayton walked into the classroom, his eyes were drawn to the blond woman sitting directly in front of the lectern. She sat cross-legged, the slit of her skirt fallen away from an expanse of thigh that ended at a blue fringe of panties. Her legs were bare. Arthur smiled as if some great mystery of the universe had been revealed to him alone. This was the Beatrice Dante had never known but only imagined. Chaucer's Blanche. Isolde the Fair.

"Thank God for lecterns," he thought, putting down his briefcase and rummaging through it for the class roster that Connie, the department secretary, had handed him earlier that afternoon. He called out the names, putting a check mark after each: Allen Bateman (small, blond boy, thick glasses); Jeff Bruce; Mark Ciolla (tall, muscular, black hair like an Elvis impersonator; hadn't he heard that the fifties were over? So were the sixties and seventies, for that matter); Steven Crow; Nancy Gerding (chubby girl, face like an apple); Samantha Kreuger.

"Present."

At the sound of her voice, bells tinkled. The songs of birds filled the room. The fragrance of roses and lilies floated past. Strange figures arranged themselves around the smiling Samantha: Lancelot, head bowed, armor gleaming; Tristan, eyes fired with passion. At the rear of the classroom, a naked man with a silver bow and a quiver full of arrows smiled satirically and sent a bolt flying directly at Arthur's chest.

Arthur touched the place where the fantasy arrow had struck and blinked back the vision.

"Emily Morrison," he continued.

When he had finished calling the role, distributing the schedule, and summarizing the course requirements, he gathered his notes and began the lecture.

"Love," he intoned, "according to Andreas Capellanus, 'is a certain inborn suffering derived from the sight of and exclusive meditation upon the beauty of the opposite sex, which causes each one to wish above all things the embrace of the other and by common desire to carry out all of love's precepts in each other's embrace.' The more perceptive among you will note that what we have here is a classic definition of sexual passion, with its emphasis on the suffering and on the sense experience, rather than on the more conventional Medieval Christian definition of love as the natural inclination of the spirit toward the good."

Arthur elaborated upon this basic idea, stressing the inevitable connection between passion (i.e., love) and death, and the perennial fascination of humankind for the forbidden, the taboo. The myopic boy seemed to be copying the lecture verbatim. The apple-faced girl giggled every few minutes, and the boy with the Elvis haircut slouched in his seat and made strenuous efforts to look bored. Arthur's eyes drifted back to Samantha Kreuger's thighs. Pink. Smooth. Lovely. His mouth went dry. He paused to check his notes, then went on.

"Romantic love has several important characteristics. First, it results from sudden illumination, the first view of the beloved, or love at first sight, as we normally think of it. Second, it is adulterous by nature, and therefore must remain secret from the rest of the world. Third, it thrives on difficulty and frustration. The more obstacles the lovers have to overcome, the more intense the love experience will be. And fourth, it raises the lovers to a new level of existence, gives them, for all practical purposes, a mystical experience."

Samantha sat with her feet together and her knees slightly apart. The blue triangle of her panties became visible for a moment.

"Um...uh... That's enough for tonight. We'll...uh...see how these characteristics work next week in Gottfried's *Tristan*."

Arthur rushed to put his notes away. Samantha glided past him, smiled and said, "Good night," oblivious of the effect she was having on him. The apple-faced girl remained to see if she *really* had to type her papers because she didn't have a computer, or even a typewriter, and couldn't afford to have someone type them for her and had he read Mary Stewart's Merlin trilogy.

Yes, he said, she *really* had to type her papers, they had plenty of computers in the Learning Skills Center, and no, he hadn't read the Merlin trilogy.

When the room was empty, he finished packing his briefcase. The fragrance of roses and lilies lingered. He switched off the light. Soft laughter came from behind him, and he turned to see the naked man with the silver bow fading into the darkness.

All the way home, he was visited by visions of Samantha Kreuger, her goddess-like thighs, that triangular patch of blue. What bliss it would be to run his hands across those thighs, to embrace her.

"Good God," he muttered. "What am I thinking?"

It was humiliating to find himself at the age of forty-two suddenly thrust back into adolescence. He had hoped he was past all that, the exquisite torments, the sudden heat, not entirely unpleasant, that flared up at the mere thought of a woman. When he was fourteen, he and Bobby Burke used to leaf through the *New York Times Magazine* in search of bra and panty ads, which they would cut out and hide in their wallets or beneath their mattresses. On Sundays, they stationed themselves in the park to ogle the college girls. Bobby had even worked out a mathematical formula to express the relationship between the sway of a woman's hips, the shape of her buttocks, and the intensity of his erection.

Silly stuff.

But Arthur also recalled the anguish of the confessional when he admitted to Father Higney every week that he had "impure thoughts," amazingly palpable visions of Debbie Reynolds, Jane Russell, naked and randy.

"You must resist these temptations, my son," the old priest would sigh, the odor of stale wine wafting through the screen.

"Pray to the Virgin, Mother of purity, for help. She will give you aid. Say a decade of the rosary and make a good act of contrition." The wizened old hermit mumbled the prayer of absolution as Arthur whispered his Act of Contrition, then slid the panel shut.

He must have said hundreds, thousands of "Hail Marys," but the fantasies persisted: Debbie Reynolds, Jane Russell, Kim Novak, Bobby Burke's sister, the entire cheerleading squad, and the girl's basketball team.

In time he had come to believe that it was, indeed, better to marry than to burn, which for him meant that since he had married Rachel fifteen years ago, he no longer lusted after every woman he saw. It was true that on occasion it would occur to him that Arlene X or Sherry Y might be nice in bed, but generally the thought remained hypothetical, intellectual, with the emotional impact of a mathematical formula.

But now he found himself conjuring up images of Samantha's pink nipples, downy pubic hair, and feared that he might be losing his grip on reality.

Gavin and Gareth were in bed and safely asleep by the time he arrived home. Rachel mixed a bourbon and water as he hung up his overcoat and cap.

"How did it go today?" she asked when they were seated in front of the living room fire.

"Okay," he answered. "Nineteen in the Medieval course. Best enrollment I've had in that for about four years."

"What are they like?"

"Pretty attentive and eager, except for one guy who looks like an Elvis Presley impersonator. Really retrograde. There's one gal…" He took a quick gulp of his bourbon. It would hardly do to say that Samantha was the most beautiful creature he had ever seen. "…who appears to have some background for this."

He took another sip of his bourbon and changed the subject. "Cameron was on my back again today. In front of Connie, too. Reminded me that it's been three years since I've published anything. Apparently, the Hammett article wasn't scholarly enough for him."

"Good grief," said Rachel. "What does that man expect? If he stopped loading you down with so much committee work you might have time for research."

"Maybe so. But in a way he's right. Other people manage it, I don't know how. They must ignore their families or something."

"You're not other people," she reminded him, and launched into a litany of Arthur's achievements and commitments.

His thoughts wandered back to Samantha.

"Listen," he interrupted. "Let's forget about Cameron and…uh, go upstairs, huh?"

Rachel smiled and gave him a sly wink.

"Sure enough, lover. Let me shower first."

While Rachel showered, Arthur poured himself another bourbon. A pang of guilt gnawed at his stomach. It was the image of Samantha's thighs, that vivid blue patch of triangle, that had prompted him to suggest the lovemaking. He loved Rachel, but he also knew that over the years their lovemaking had become less a matter of intense passion than a simple expression of affection.

Rachel's nakedness no longer aroused him. It had become familiar. Her skin was no longer soft and supple. Lines had appeared around her eyes, her breasts sagged, she had grown slightly thick around the middle, and there were stretch marks on her abdomen. Only the softness of her touch, the playfulness of her fingers across his belly and thighs, the warmth of her breath on his face, brought him to arousal. He wondered if she thought of his flabbiness in the same way.

Visual stimuli are short-lived, he mused. Only the new, the mysterious, the forbidden excite. The first rose is the miracle. Thereafter, a rose is merely beautiful.

Later, as they caressed in the darkness, though he spoke Rachel's name, he imagined himself making love to Samantha, her eyes closed, nostrils flaring with passion, hips thrusting wildly up to meet his. When he reached his climax and fell back on the pillow, the image vanished. Rachel breathed softly, nestled her head on his shoulder, and they were soon asleep.

"'When Tristan and Isolde drank the love potion, they drank their own death.' Thus says Gottfried."

Arthur looked out over the class. Two undergraduates had already dropped the course—there was too much reading, they were already taking three English courses, and they didn't need this course to graduate, anyway. He had gladly initialed the appropriate box on their registration control forms. Everyone else had managed to endure the first two meetings, and Arthur was confident there would be no further withdrawals.

For the third week in a row, Samantha Kreuger sat directly in front of the lectern. For a moment he believed she was actively trying to seduce him, but dismissed the thought. Seating arrangements were a product of other factors: self-confidence, interest, some strange sort of territorial imperative. This was Samantha's seat, and no one else would even think of taking it. Seduction had nothing to do with it.

Tonight she was dressed in black: blouse, skirt, boots, a black mantilla draped over her hair. Though Arthur was certain such ostentation was not a matter of conscious design, it was clear that her costume had drawn everyone's attention. The apple-faced girl pursed her lips in disapproval. The myopic boy peered at her over the rim of his glasses. The Elvis clone feigned indifference, but from time to time his eyes drifted toward her, then slowly drifted away. Arthur made a conscious effort not to look at her.

"Our understanding of *Tristan*," he continued, "depends upon our interpretation of the love potion. Is the potion a real magical device which robs the lovers of their wills and makes them victims of fate? Or is it a metaphor for something else—say, some defect of character in the lovers? The issue here is whether Tristan and Isolde are manipulated by some perverse deity, or whether they are, in some respect, responsible for their own downfall because of the choices they make. What do you think?"

He waited for some response but was met with silence.
"Anyone?"

Nothing.

"Emily. How do you read this?"

A skinny girl with frizzy hair shrugged her shoulders and mumbled, "I d'know."

"Haven't thought about it much, eh? Mark?"

Elvis yawned and tapped his pencil on the desk.

"It doesn't really matter that much to me," he answered. "If Gottfried says it's a magic potion, why shouldn't I believe him?"

Arthur suppressed the urge to blurt out "Jackass," and smiled instead.

"Do you think Gottfried is being ironic?"

Elvis/Mark put his pencil down and looked out the window. "I suppose. I don't see it."

Arthur began to feel the class drifting away from him, that he was losing control. Already he could hear Cameron's stentorian voice berating him: "Clayton, you're incompetent. Your student evaluations are abysmal, and you can't even get a decent discussion going."

Arthur allowed himself to look once again at Samantha. She smiled up at him as if everything he had to say were of immense interest to her. Perhaps she could save him.

"How about it, Samantha. What do you think?"

"I think Tristan and Isolde are just plain horny."

Laughter rippled through the classroom. Her response thrilled Arthur as if she had agreed to sleep with him.

"No, really," she continued, uncrossing her legs and searching through her copy of the romance. "They are sexually attracted to each other before they even take the love potion. Look at what Tristan says on page 150 when he tells Mark about her. 'Her beauty makes others beautiful.' The entire passage shows that he's interested in her. Then on 173 when she sees him in the bath, Gottfried says this: 'She stole glance after glance at his hands and face, she studied his arms and legs, which so openly proclaimed what he tried to keep so secret.' It's plain to me what she's looking at."

Arthur suddenly felt as naked as Tristan in his bath and circled back behind the lectern.

"So your position is?" he said.

"That Tristan and Isolde don't really need the potion. It's just an excuse."

"Then you see the potion as a metaphor?"

"Definitely," she answered.

"A metaphor for what?"

"Well," she began, then paused as if to make sure that she phrased what she had to say correctly. "I guess for the passion which they let take over."

Several hands shot up.

Thank God, he thought. My salvation.

The debate became quite lively, and by the time the class ended, Samantha had acquitted herself admirably, in Arthur's estimation.

When the room was empty, he packed his briefcase and muttered, "Screw you, Cameron." Incompetent, indeed. In spite of everything, it had gone well and would continue to go well. Samantha was a formidable debater, willing to take a position and defend it. Moreover, she liked him. He could see it in her smile, hear it in the enthusiasm with which she argued a point.

Her apparition materialized before him in the darkened classroom. "I'm in love with you," it whispered, and placed his hand on her breast.

"Easy does it, Clayton," he said, and was alone again. His palm still tingled from the ghostly touch.

The following morning, he encountered Samantha in the corridor outside his office.

"Dr. Clayton. If you have some time, I'd like to discuss an idea I have for the Tristan paper."

The slight musk in her perfume made him lightheaded, and he answered, much too abruptly, he thought, "Not right now. I'm rather busy."

It was not what he wanted to say. More than ever, he wanted to talk with her, to have her next to him, enfolded in that musky fragrance, to drink in every detail of her. But her presence made him uncomfortably aware that he was losing control. He hoped he hadn't insulted her.

"Will tomorrow morning about nine do?" he added.

"It will do wonderfully," she said. "See you then."

Entranced by the sway of her hips, Arthur watched her down the corridor.

Without warning the fantasy began to play itself: Samantha turned, desire burning in her eyes, and beckoned to him. He followed, helpless, willing to do anything she said, down to the copier room where, completely clothed, they fulfilled their passion atop the Xerox machine, generating ream after ream of paper to the rhythm of their lovemaking.

When the fantasy had exhausted itself, he found himself alone in the corridor. The fragrance of her perfume lingered. Roses and lilies. He was sweating.

How many more times in the next several weeks such fantasies played themselves, he couldn't have said, but they came in the middle of lectures or as he sat correcting papers. Gradually, he began to feel she had cast some sort of spell or slipped him a magic potion. "Unreasonable," he argued with himself. She could not control his body chemistry. She was simply there. "It is all a matter of which shall have the mastery: the mind or the body."

One evening over dinner, her face appeared in his soup, hovered over the meat loaf, and came to rest at the edge of his plate.

"You okay, hon?" Rachel asked.

The room dissolved, the room gathered itself once again.

"It's nothing. Cameron again. Informed me today that I wouldn't be promoted to full unless my publications are more scholarly. In his mind, Hammett and Chandler aren't worth writing about."

It was a lie. Not the conversation, of course. That had really happened. But what was bothering him was a lie. How could he tell Rachel he was having an erotic fantasy about another woman, especially a younger woman in her twenties? One of his students, at that? She would never believe it was nothing more than a fantasy. So he lied.

At two-thirty in the morning, Rachel snoring gently beside him, he still lay wide awake, visions of Samantha swimming around the room. He climbed out of bed and went to the kitchen. As the milk warmed on the stove, he picked up a pencil and doodled on a piece of scratch paper. The doodles became the name "Samantha" traced over and over until it nearly wore through the paper.

He poured the milk into a cup and spooned in the chocolate. It occurred to him he might write a poem, the first since his undergraduate days: a poem for Samantha, which he would keep safely hidden somewhere. Perhaps that would solve the problem, get things out of his system.

He sat at the table and wrote, "A garden grows behind your smile." He studied the line a moment, crossed out the word "smile," and wrote above it the word "eyes," then went on: "Where lovely roses bloom." He set the pencil down and read the lines through several times. He placed the poem in an ashtray and set fire to it.

The hot chocolate was beginning to relax him, and as the ashes of his poem smoldered in the ashtray, Arthur was aware of someone standing behind him. He turned to find himself looking up at Samantha.

Her eyes were half closed, her lips were parted and quivering. Her breasts were white and creamy, and the golden triangle of hair between her thighs sparkled like the sun. She stretched her arms toward him, and in an instant they were rolling back and forth across the kitchen table. In another instant, something inside him exploded, and he felt himself rushing down a long tunnel. The tunnel walls were painted with naked figures, great lovers of legend: Tristan and Isolde, Lancelot and Guinevere, Troilus and Criseyde, Venus and Adonis.

Arthur and Samantha.

He came to rest in the middle of a garden. Birds sang overhead, the strains of lute music floated in the air. Roses, daisies, lilies surrounded him. In the garden's center, a pure white fountain spouted silvery jets of water that ran over the edges and formed a stream that coursed past his feet. Two white bulls and a spotted bull cavorted by a hedge of thorns. Before he could take a single step, it was night and he was seated on a log before a small fire.

An aged hermit in rags stirred gruel in a small pot over the fire. His face was pallid and gaunt, his hands ashen and gnarled. From time to time he glanced up at Arthur and muttered "Ave Maria." At length, he stopped stirring the gruel, ladled some into a cracked wooden bowl, and seated himself cross-legged in front of the fire.

"I shall expound to you the meaning of this vision," began the hermit. He raised the bowl to his lips, drained it, wiped his mouth on a gritty sleeve, belched, and continued.

"The two white bulls represent Galahad and Percival, maidens clean and without spot. The spotted bull represents Sir Bors de Ganis who trespassed once in his virginity, but who since has kept himself so chaste that all is forgiven him. These three alone shall achieve the grail. You are the black bull, so steeped in sin, a heart so full of lust, you shall never achieve the grail."

The old man spat into the fire. Arthur leaped up to protest, but as he did, the ground lurched and he pitched forward.

He was back in the kitchen staring into the navel of the naked man with the silver bow. The man, tall, muscular, with a curly brown beard and hair all over his body, tested the point of a golden arrow with the tip of his thumb.

"Who are you? What do you want?" Arthur asked.

"I want nothing. What you want," said the man, gesturing with his arrow toward Arthur's groin, "is fairly obvious."

Arthur crossed his legs.

"As to who I am, some call me Eros, some call me Cupid. The Renaissance portrayed me as a cherubic little creature with wings. Sentimental crap. I am as you see me."

The man completed his examination of the arrow and offered it to Arthur for inspection.

"A fine shaft, wouldn't you say? One hundred percent effective."

Arthur recoiled from the offer.

"But of course you know that."

"Leave me alone," Arthur snapped.

"Ah, I see the problem. Unrequited love, disdainful lady and all that. You need my help, professor."

"I need you to stop tormenting me."

The naked man sneered at Arthur.

"Self-pity? Unbecoming. If you wish the torment to end, you must do something about it, take matters into your own hands, uh, so to speak. Confess yourself, make an end of it. Tell Samantha of your undying love for her."

"I'm a married man," protested Arthur.

"Marriage is no excuse for not loving."

"I love my wife."

"It is a well known fact that love cannot exist between husband and wife."

"But these things have consequences. Broken marriages. Damaged children."

"Cross that bridge when you come to it."

"Damn it," said Arthur, slamming his fist on the table. "You're talking about animal passion, desire, a chimera. It cannot last."

"Balls," said the naked man glaring at Arthur. "It comes down to this, professor. Are you content to have Samantha only in dreams? To wonder for the rest of your life what it really would have been like? It's time for action, professor. Fish or cut bait."

Arthur looked down at his hands and closed his eyes. When he opened them, early morning sunlight streamed through the kitchen window. The naked man was gone. The clock on the stove read five minutes to seven. Rachel would be down shortly to fix breakfast and get the boys ready for school. He splashed cold water on his face and poured a glass of juice to wash the sour taste from his mouth. Despite a slight backache, he felt calm and relaxed, as if he had passed through some crisis and come out on the other side whole. It's only in your head, he thought as he drained the juice.

The morning went smoothly. For a change, all of his first year writing students were prepared, and most of the people in the short story class had read the day's assignment. He even managed, after returning from his classes, to type a few handouts before noon. Not once had he thought about Samantha. It was as if last night's dream had been some sort of purgative. After lunch, he made some notes for his Malory lecture and was about to correct some essays when Samantha appeared at the office door.

"I'm so glad you're here," she bubbled. "Do you have some time?"

"Certainly," he said. "Come in. Sit down."

She removed her coat and draped it over the back of a chair, then sat down and crossed her legs. The collar of her navy blue blouse was open enough to reveal a shadow of cleavage that set Arthur's blood racing.

"I'm almost ready to type," she began, "but wanted to discuss a few things to make sure I was on the right track."

As she explained her thesis that the quest for the grail was a sexual quest, and that the grail itself was a symbol for the female genitals raised to the level of spirit, Arthur found himself entranced with the curve of her throat, the tilt of her head, the roundness of her breasts. Though the argument, he thought, was misplaced Freudianism, her breasts were lovely.

Before he was aware of it, she lifted her head and their eyes met, their gazes locked.

They couldn't have looked at each other very long, surely no more than two or three seconds, probably less, but in that time he knew, as certainly as he could know anything, that the affair had been consummated though he had never even touched her. She leaned back in the chair, a half smile playing across her face.

"Well," she said. "What do you suppose we should do now?"

"Do?"

"I know what that look means, professor."

"Look?"

"You want to go to bed with me, get into my pants."

Good God, he thought. Is it that obvious?

"You've been looking at me that way all semester."

He wanted to deny everything, to claim a purely aesthetic interest, but she would never believe that and, he was quite sure, would think the less of him for it. He wished he could be any place but here. Even Cameron couldn't make him feel this uncomfortable.

"In fact," she said, "I'm surprised it's taken you so long."

"Time to make an end of it," whispered Eros. "Confess yourself to her."

He ignored the voice, denied the image of the naked man that was beginning to take shape behind her. "I think you've got the wrong idea," he began.

"I don't have the wrong idea. You're just horny, is all."

Arthur was dismayed at the direction the conversation was taking. He half wished she were infuriated. She should storm out of the office. Report him to Cameron. To the dean. File sexual harassment charges. At the very least, she should slap his face. Then the confrontation would be at an end. But there she sat, running the thumb and forefinger of her left hand along the collar of her blouse, her eyes looking directly into his.

"Really, Samantha. I don't know what to say. I mean, you're very attractive, and…" He paused, not sure where he was going with this.

"Don't stop now," said the naked man. "A word or two more and she's yours. Tonight."

"I enjoy sex, too," she said, and smiled. "It's perfectly natural. I'm not one of those radical feminists who hate men. I like men. I like you. You're a very sweet man."

Arthur leaned forward with his forearm on the desk, his hands fluttering like wounded pigeons.

"Listen. I don't think this is a good idea."

"Of course, you don't."

"I mean, I'm a married man. I love my wife, my children."

"I'm not looking to break up your marriage, Arthur. I'm not going to take pictures, or post it on the net, or anything like that. It might be fun."

He cleared his throat. "This sort of thing is not possible."

"Not possible?" said the naked man. "What do you mean not possible? Anything is possible."

"Not possible. I mean that these things have consequences, devastating consequences—on wives, on children, on families."

"Come on, Arthur. We're not talking about love, anyway. We're just talking about sex. Nobody will ever know," said Samantha. "It will be our secret."

"But I'd know. My body would give me away. Rachel would figure it out. Maybe not that I was seeing someone, but that something was wrong, something was different. And then she'd ask me and I'd tell her because I never have been able to lie to her."

"Crap," said the naked man. "What a load of crap." He reached out and tapped Samantha on the shoulder with one of his golden arrows. She shivered briefly, then looked more beautiful to Arthur than she ever had before. Samantha's hair shone more golden than it ever had. Her lips were brighter, redder, wetter, asking to be kissed. And her nipples seemed to be pressing against the smooth, blue fabric of her blouse.

"Look at her, professor. Such a delicious morsel. She's yours, all yours for the asking. Carpe diem, professor. Seize the day. Now."

"I'm Catholic, for Christ's sake."

"Me, too," she said. "You can go to confession."

"That's not funny."

"I know," she said. "I'm sorry. But the fact is, you're making too big a thing of this."

He found himself looking down at his hands, at the papers on his desk, afraid that if he looked at Samantha, all of his resolve would melt and he would go with her. There was a silence, then Samantha shifted in her chair and stood up.

"I suppose you need time to think about it, sort things out. We don't need to do it tonight. Maybe we can go for coffee after class tomorrow. We can discuss my paper then," she said. "And other things."

When he looked up, Samantha had put on her coat and was picking up her books. He watched in silence as she turned to leave.

When she reached the door, she turned and said, "You really are a sweet man."

There was nothing he could say, and as the echo of her heels receded down the corridor, he knew how Lancelot must have felt to be led to the grail castle only to have the ultimate vision denied to him at the last moment.

"Well, professor," said the naked man. "You blew it."

"Shut up," Arthur grumbled.

He sat without moving for what seemed an hour. A sweet man. Samantha had called him a sweet man. Arthur Clayton, the noble, the virtuous. Just once he would like to break loose and do something hideous. Pop Cameron on the nose. Put a brick through a window in the administration building. Fall deeply in bed with someone like Samantha. But somehow it was not like him, did not fit the image. Sweet man.

He had not fallen today. Today he had resisted temptation, the call of the flesh. Father Higney would be proud. But it was no real victory. It didn't even come close to that. It wasn't his virtue that had saved him, not the struggle of his spirit upward to overcome his own lecherous leanings. It was something more base, more cowardly. It was fear that had saved him: fear that he would get caught, fear that Rachel would find out, that Cameron would find out, that his kids would know, that everyone in the world would be made aware Arthur Clayton was not the tower of virtue and probity he pretended to be, aspired to be. At base, he wasn't any different than the millions of men the feminists wrote about, who couldn't see women beyond their own genital needs. He wanted to be more than that; he prayed to the God in whom, on most days, he only half believed that he *could* be more. But, for now, all he had was the fear to protect him, and he didn't know if fear would be enough.

First Step

He pushed her down on the bed so hard she cracked her head against the wall. Light exploded behind her eyes. Bobbie prayed she would lose consciousness so she wouldn't know what was happening. But she didn't. He forced himself between her thighs and ripped her underpants away and stuffed them in her mouth so she couldn't scream. Then he hit her across the face. Her cheeks burned. All of his weight fell on her and he pounded into her. As he moved, Bobbie felt as if great chunks of her were being ripped away, fistful by fistful, and she wanted to hold onto them, bring them back and scream, but she was afraid he would hit her again or, worse, do something to her babies.

When he collapsed on top of her, she felt like retching, the smell of sweat, beer, and gasoline from the car he had been working on was so strong. She gagged on her underpants. He rolled away and pulled them out of her mouth. She gasped in a lungful of air, shuddered, turned onto her side, her back toward him, and bit the thumb-knuckle of her left hand until she tasted blood.

The springs creaked as he stood up.

He padded across the floor, belched, and closed the bathroom door behind him.

Bobbie buried her face in the pillow and cried. God, she hated him. Before they were married, he used to do handstands for her after he'd had a couple of beers, and she'd giggle like crazy when all of the cigarettes tumbled out of his shirt pocket. Now she wished he would die and leave her alone.

The toilet flushed. The door squeaked open.

He was standing over her, staring, his eyes boring into her back. She squeezed her eyes shut and prayed he would go away.

"What are you blubbering about?"

She didn't answer, couldn't answer. If she said anything, he'd call her a liar and hit her the way he always did when he was drunk. She prayed he wouldn't hit her for saying nothing.

"How come you always cry when I make love to you anymore? You think I'm not good enough for you? You think I'm too rough? You used to like it rough."

He grabbed her by the arm, his fingers pressing through the flesh until they almost touched bone, and yanked her from the bed. She hit the floor, but he held her and she thought he was going to pull her arm from its socket.

"It's that social worker putting ideas in your head." He started twisting her arm and pushed his face toward hers. "I bet you're doing him, aren't you? Isn't that it?"

"No, Austin," she sobbed, trying to pull away from his grip. "I swear to God I haven't done anything."

He let go and she fell to the floor. The children started to cry in the next room. He loomed over her, his fist cocked, ready to strike. He looked to her like the giant in a fairy tale, the one that chased her screaming from dreams.

"I find out you're doing him," said Austin, leaning forward, his breath beery and stale, "I'm gone to lock you up again."

She covered her face with her hands. He pulled his pants on and lurched through the bedroom door toward the kitchen. She heard him yell at the babies to shut up, then pop the tab of a beer can. The babies screamed louder.

She didn't want to be locked up a second time, refused to be locked up again. It was worse than his hitting her. The first time, he'd tied her hands behind her back with lamp cord, and tied her feet together and tossed her naked in the closet, her mouth taped so she couldn't yell out. He'd left her in there so long she'd pissed herself twice and had to lie in her own piss 'til it turned rancid.

When he let her out, she shook all over, and her muscles were so knotted up she could barely stand. He told her it served her right for not doing what she was told. But it didn't serve her right, and she wouldn't let him do that again.

The screen door banged closed.

She stumbled into the bathroom and looked at herself in the mirror. Her eyes were puffy and red; her face was streaked red where he had slapped her. Her hair was mousy and matted with sweat. Her mouth looked swollen, though she knew it was not. She started to cry again as she remembered how pretty she had been when he'd asked her to marry him. She wasn't pretty anymore. She hated him for making her not pretty.

She washed her face, then put on shorts and a T-shirt. Her left arm hurt from when he had pulled her off the bed. She went into the kitchen. The babies were still crying. She put a bottle of formula on the stove to warm for Rachel, and gave Aaron a bottle of apple juice. Then she changed their diapers. Aaron's were just wet. Rachel had filled hers and was getting a rash.

Austin was in the yard, shirtless, barefoot, a cigarette dangling from the corner of his mouth. His right arm hung loose at his side; his hand clutched a short-handled axe. He raised the axe, sighted down the handle, cocked his arm back and threw. The axe blade buried itself in a tree with a dull "chunk." Austin drank the last of his beer without taking the cigarette from his mouth, then tossed the empty beer can over his shoulder.

"Bobbie," he yelled at the house.

She went to the screen door and looked out.

"I need another beer, babe." He smiled at her as if everything were all right, as if everything were normal, as if he'd never hit her or slapped her or locked her in the closet. Then he walked over to the tree and worked the axe up and down until it came out.

She went to the refrigerator and took out a can of beer.

"Chunk," went the axe in the tree.

She popped the top off the can and carried it out to him. He grinned at her the same way he'd grinned at her six years ago at carnival time when he'd asked her to marry him—boyish, naive, innocent. He took the can from her, grabbed her around the waist and pulled her to him and kissed her so hard she felt as if he were trying to break her jaw. He let go of her and said, his voice softened, "You know I love you, don't you, Bobbie?"

"Yeah, I know," she said. "I've got to feed the kids."

She went back to the house. Rachel was screaming for her bottle. She held Rachel in her arms, placed the nipple between the infant's lips.

"Chunk," went the axe in the tree.

Mr. Beale, the social worker, sat at the kitchen table, the coffee cup in one hand, a pencil in the other. He was jotting things down in a little spiral notebook he carried in his shirt pocket. Austin was at the gas station, working. Either that, or at the bar.

"Are you all right?" Mr. Beale said.

"I'm okay," she said.

"Are you sure?"

She looked up from the ironing board.

"Yes."

Mr. Beale's eyes met hers, probed deeply, looking for the truth behind her words. His eyes were green and gentle. She felt her face turn warm and looked away from him.

He sipped his coffee. "It's getting worse, isn't it?"

She didn't look up, but pushed the iron back and forth across the pillowcase she was working on. "There's nothing wrong."

"Where did you get the bruises?"

"Accident." She didn't know what else to say. If she told him the truth and Austin found out… She bit her lower lip and focused on the iron.

"What about the kids?"

"The kids are okay, too."

Mr. Beale tapped the eraser end of his pencil against the tabletop.

"You know it's only a matter of time before he goes after one of the kids."

She put the iron down and looked directly at him.

"He wouldn't dare go after the kids. He loves the kids."

Mr. Beale looked directly back at her, and for a moment she thought that he really was a handsome man. Her face started to get warm again.

He began writing something on a slip of paper he had torn out of his notebook.

"There's a shelter on Prince Street. He can't get you there."

"I don't think so," she said. "I don't want to talk about it anymore."

"You'll have to take the first step sometime, Bobbie. It can only get worse. Here's the number." He slid the paper across the table toward her. "Memorize it so you don't have to fish around for it in an emergency. Call anytime, day or night. Someone will come and get you."

"I can take care of myself." She unplugged the cord and wrapped it around the handle of the iron. Then she took Mr. Beale's empty coffee cup and put it in the sink. "I have to get the kids' lunch now."

When he was gone, she sat alone in the kitchen and looked at the slip of paper Mr. Beale had given her. She said the phone number out loud three or four times. There was an address on the paper, and she said that out loud three or four times, too. Then she tore the paper into tiny fragments and tossed them into the trashcan under the sink.

She wondered what it would be like to be married to Mr. Beale. She bet he wouldn't beat his wife or lock her up in the closet. Someone like Mr. Beale would treat her with respect, would let her go to college.

Why couldn't Austin be like that? He used to be. He was so sweet the night he proposed. He'd had about three or four beers and was doing handstands for her. Even now, she could still see him on the midway, the Ferris wheel in the background turning the night around, his feet in the air, his hands taking one step after the other like a camel. She'd giggled like crazy when all his cigarettes tumbled out of his shirt pocket. Then he collapsed in laughter, and when the laughter subsided, he lay there looking up at her, the crowd stepping around him, and said, "So you gone to marry me, or what?"

She'd told him she wanted to go to college to improve herself, first, maybe even become a doctor – her counselor said she could do it – and he'd squeezed her arm and told her, "You don't need to go to college. You got me. I'll give you all the improving you need."

She'd told him she would have to think about it, and she might have said "No" if her parents hadn't raised such a fuss. They didn't like Austin Cleary at all, said he was scum, that he came from scum and would always be scum. They'd said that about every boy she had ever liked. Even Father Travis, who she thought was on her side, said he believed she could do better. "At least," Father Travis had said, "before you make a final decision, let's pray about it together."

In the end, she had married Austin as much out of spite as out of love. But she had loved him. He was lively, unrestrained. He made her laugh.

She wanted to love him the way she used to, but it was hard to love him through all that pain and humiliation.

Maybe something would happen to him on the way home. Maybe he'd have an accident, get hit by a truck, drive himself into the canal. If he were dead…

How could she think such things? It was Austin. She was even thinking like him. So she hated him for making her hate him so much she could think like that.

When he came home later, he was drunk. She couldn't remember when he'd been sober last. It was at least three, four days. He took a beer from the refrigerator and sat crying on the living room sofa, crying the way he had when his band fell apart. That was the last time she'd seen him happy, while the band was still together. After that, everything changed.

Bobbie stood shivering in the doorway. She knew the self-pity, recognized it as the start of something worse. Whatever had happened, he would blame her for it.

He looked up at her, his knees spread, the beer can resting against his crotch.

"He fired me. That sonofabitching Earl fired me. Said I was drunk." He took a swallow of beer. "I look drunk to you?"

She shook her head. If she tried to talk, she would cry. He stared at her, pushed himself up from the sofa, almost fell back down, but corrected his balance.

"You look at me like I'm some kind of bug. You think I'm drunk, too."

He lurched toward her and stopped directly in front of her. His hand went to her neck and he pressed his thumb against her jawbone. She closed her eyes, afraid he was going to strangle her, praying he would do it quickly, so she couldn't feel the pain. Then the pressure was gone and she opened her eyes to see him lurch through the kitchen and out the back door. She could hear the sound of the axe chunking into the tree.

She tried to block the chunking sound from her mind as she made dinner. She didn't know what he would do, but she knew he was going to do something. Beat her. Lock her in the closet. She wouldn't let him do it. She'd kill him rather than go back in the closet.

As she chopped the onions, she found herself crying and saying over and over, "I don't want him to hit me again. God, please don't let him hit me again."

The chunking sound stopped.

The screen door banged shut.

She turned, wiped the stinging tears from her eyes, and found him standing there. He swayed as if the breeze were blowing him, but otherwise he didn't move. He grinned at her.

The axe dangled from his right hand.

He looked at her as if she were the tree. She tried to say something, his name, anything, but nothing would come.

"He was here today," he said.

"Who?"

"That social worker. Beale."

"Yes, but..."

"You let him do you, didn't you?"

"No, Austin, I…"

"Don't lie to me." He twisted her left arm behind her, pushed it up as far as it would go, and held the axe blade to her throat. "I can smell him all over you. You let him do you because you think he's gentle and I'm a piece of crap."

"Austin, please." It was getting hard to breathe. He must have vomited at some point, for the odor of beer and vomit settled over her like a wet cloth. She tried to breathe.

"I'm not so dumb I don't know what you think of me. I don't like you looking at me like I was some kind of bug. You always look at me like I was some kind of bug. Now you're letting that social worker do you. I don't like that. I hate that. I'm going to do something about that."

He pressed the axe blade against her cheek. It was cold. She'd never felt anything so cold.

"But not now." He pushed her away from him. He held the axe up so she could see it. "Not now. Sometime when you're not looking. Sometime when you're not expecting it. Maybe when you're sleeping."

He laughed. He took another beer from the refrigerator and staggered into the living room.

She fumbled everything as she got supper ready. She browned the onions in the skillet, broke up the hamburger, dropping some of it on the floor, cut herself on the can opener as she opened the tomato sauce. She sucked on her thumb until the bleeding stopped. The rice stuck in the pan. She was crying the whole time, convulsions rumbling through her chest, making her tremble all over.

It wasn't going to be the closet this time. This time…

He was going to kill her. She knew it. He'd said he was going to kill her before, but this time he was going to do it. The other times he'd said it as a joke to frighten her, keep her in line. This time she knew he wasn't joking. Sooner or later he would take the axe to her and then to her babies. God, not the babies.

He was going to do it after supper, while she was clearing away the dishes, putting them in the sink. He would sneak up behind her while her hands were in the wash water, and smash her head in. He'd leave her slumped over the sink, probably with her head pushed into the water, and go after Rachel and Aaron.

She clapped her hands to her mouth and squeezed her eyes shut. She couldn't let him do that. Not to her. Not to the babies.

With trembling hands, she set the food on the table, trying to think of what she could do.

She called Austin for supper.

There was no answer.

She called again. There was still no answer.

A tremor ran through her as she thought that he was playing another joke on her, that he wanted her to come into the living room after him so he could jump out at her with the axe and scare her to death before he killed her.

Cautiously, she approached the door. There was no movement in the living room. Through the doorway she could see, reflected in the mirror on the wall, Austin slumped on the couch, his chin on his chest, snoring. The can of beer rested loosely in his fingers. He had set the axe on the end table beside the couch.

"Austin," she called, at first in a whisper, then a second time, a bit louder. There was no reaction. Rachel began to cry softly in the bedroom.

Bobbie walked through the doorway and over to the couch. She touched Austin lightly on the shoulder.

"Austin, it's supper."

No answer. He'd passed out. He'd be out for three or four hours. She felt something drop away from her, a weight or a set of chains.

Her hands shook as she removed the half-empty beer can from his fingers as gently as she could and placed it on the end table. Her eyes fell on the axe.

She brushed her fingers across the wooden handle. It was smooth, almost as smooth as the silk blouse she wore the night

Austin had asked her to marry him. It was the axe he was going to kill her with.

She wrapped her fingers around the wooden handle and lifted it. It was lighter than she expected it to be, lighter than her skillet. She gripped the handle in her right hand, let the blade rest in the palm of her left. The blade was cold, and there were a few nicks in it, but it was sharp.

It was the axe he was going to kill her with. When he awoke three or four hours later, it wouldn't matter that he had passed out. He would accuse her of drugging him and come after her.

She would have to do something sooner or later. She had to protect her babies, to protect herself.

She ran her thumb along the blade of the axe and watched Austin's face. She couldn't do it with him facing her. That would be too awful. It would remind her too much of how wildly in love she had been with him once, and how a small part of her still loved him, wanted him to be something other than what he was, wanted to bring back the days when he did handstands and played in the band. It reminded her of her own failure: if she loved him enough, he wouldn't beat her or lock her in the closet or want to kill her.

She stood behind him and studied the back of his neck, the shaggy curling of his blond hair, and thought of the beatings and the violence and the pain. She thought of the humiliation of being locked naked in a closet with her hands tied behind her.

She thought of the humiliation of being raped by her own husband.

The hatred built up in her, surged through her stomach, her chest, her arms. She raised the axe high above her head, ready to bring it crashing down on his skull so it would be over.

Rachel screeched in the bedroom.

Bobbie jerked her head around and saw herself reflected in the mirror, the axe poised above her head, her face pale and lifeless. Austin's face. It was Austin walking around inside her, Austin with the axe ready to strike.

Her muscles relaxed, her arms fell to her sides. The axe dropped to the floor. She stared at the back of his neck, aware that when he woke, he would come after her, would always come after her, would try to kill her. If he could find her.

She went to the bedroom and dressed the babies.

The Beast

The sand burned his feet. His mother spread the blanket and told him to stand on it until she unpacked everything. Then she had him take his clothes off and put his bathing suit on. His father would take him into the water in a few minutes.

"But I don't want to go in the water, Mommy. I want to stay here with you."

"Don't be silly. Daddy will be with you, and I have to stay here with your sister."

"But I'm scared of the water, Mommy."

"That's ridiculous. There's nothing to be frightened of. Besides, Daddy won't let anything happen."

He looked out at the water. The ocean was vast and frightening to him. It was so large, so endless, so restless. The waves made a loud growling noise as they crashed against the shore, as if they were some huge beast hungry for little boy. And the water was red with seaweed, blood red. All kinds of things could happen.

His father had to practically drag him down to the water, and he could feel himself becoming more and more terrified. He tried to pull away from his father's grip, but his father held on and pulled him toward the water.

"I don't want to go, Daddy. Please don't make me go. I'll be good. I promise."

"Don't be such a baby. The water won't hurt you. Come on. We'll just stand in it for a minute."

He stood in water up to his ankles. The water rushed forward, splashing up against his shins, then receded, tugging at his ankles like hands trying to drag him away. His father held his wrist so he couldn't fall (or run away). Then his father pushed him forward until he was waist high in the water, and all he could hear was the rushing of the ocean.

He tried to break away, but his father just held him more firmly. Then his father lifted him by the armpits and carried him forward until the water was up to his father's waist. He started to scream, "I don't want to go. I don't want to go," and kicked his feet against the water, but his father wouldn't listen. He twisted around and tried to grab his father's arm, but his father held him around the waist.

"Come on, son. This is fun. You're going to be okay."

He turned back in time to see an enormous wave bearing down on them, large as a mountain, and looming over them like some craven beast, its fangs anxious for little boy flesh. In another moment it was upon them, and his father's arm slipped easily, carelessly away from his stomach as he felt himself being pulled away from his parents, away from the world, away from life, and down into the depths of the beast. He opened his mouth to scream, but sea water filled his mouth, his lungs, pushed up his nose and into his ears, had its way with him, tumbling him over and over and over, his hands thrashing out and grabbing clumps of seaweed like great tufts of fur from the body of the beast.

Then a hand grabbed his hand and pulled him to his feet, and he was choking and vomiting seawater as his father laughed and yelled, "That sure was a big one, wasn't it?" The sea still tugged at him, his chest, his legs, trying to draw him back to it, to savor the taste of little boy—couldn't his father see that?—and he struggled against his father's hand, trying desperately to get back to the safety of sand and blanket.

"Son. Stop. You just swallowed a little seawater is all. It's no big deal."

He broke from his father's grip and stumbled through the water toward the shore. His mother was standing at the edge of the water. He threw his arms around her and choked and cried.

"It's all right," she said. "It's all right." Her hand patted the back of his head and he felt safe again. The beast of the sea was now beyond his reach and could not get him, could not eat him. Not today.

The Spirit of Things

Ben Ryan hadn't had a decent night's sleep in nearly three weeks. There were too many noises: mice scratching in the walls, the grandfather clock in the hall ticking much too loudly (it never occurred to him to remove the weights so it wouldn't run), doors and windows rattling because the house was so drafty, floorboards creaking. Worst of all was the owl that perched in the maple outside his window and hooted from ten at night until a half hour before dawn.

He set out boxes of D-Con to take care of the mice, and that seemed to work fairly well, except the mice died in the walls and the house started to stink. He spent the better part of a week caulking windows and doors to keep out the drafts, and that seemed to work, too. The doors and windows rattled less, but the floorboards still creaked.

The owl was another story. Ryan had hoped it would kill itself by eating a poisoned mouse, but the owl either had an uncanny sense of which mice were poisoned and avoided them, or had some strange capacity to absorb poison without being affected.

When the owl didn't die, Ben stationed himself beneath the tree and pelted the bird with rocks. The first rock glanced off a branch and struck Ben on the right shoulder. The second whizzed past the bird and crashed through the bedroom window.

The following morning as he replaced the pane of glass, he decided to keep things simple and shoot the damned bird. He'd run into town later and buy a gun.

He wiped the excess putty from his knife into the can and stepped back to see what the window looked like. The whole frame would have to be painted over, and you could tell which was the new pane of glass because the rest were cloudy with old age. But that would do for now.

Downstairs, he put the can of putty, the putty knife, the hammer, and the screwdriver on the side of the kitchen sink, rinsed his hands under cold water, and dried them.

The phone cricketed. It was one of those phones Radio Shack sold for nine dollars, cheaply produced, but useful. He picked it up.

"Ben?" The voice at the other end sounded as if it were speaking through a tin can.

"Adrienne? Hi. I'm glad you called." He tried to sound cheerful, but to himself at least sounded merely hysterical.

"I called to remind you," she said.

"About what?"

There was a silence. "You've forgotten, haven't you?"

What had he forgotten? Dinner with her? A mortgage payment? A birthday? Kevin. Something to do with Kevin.

"Kevin's last game?" she said. "My God, Ben, he's pitching tonight."

"Come on, Ade. It slipped my mind is all. I would have remembered," he said, thinking that he wouldn't have remembered if she hadn't called. "I really would have."

"You still...oh, never mind."

"I forgot. I'm sorry. Okay? Where is it?"

"The field next to the high school, if you can find that. Where it always is."

"I can find it all right."

There was a click at the other end of the line.

He slammed the phone back into the holder.

"Damn," he said, and the house whispered "damn" back at him.

He loved his son, loved him fiercely, savagely, and had really tried to be a concerned and loving father. But somehow the years had passed, the boy had turned fifteen, and Ben realized that in that time he had been to only a handful of Kevin's activities.

He had seen Kevin play ball once, when Kevin was ten. He hadn't seen Kevin play at all this year, and here it was, the last day of the season, and Kevin was pitching. Ben couldn't miss this game.

His eyes wandered across the kitchen, the worn linoleum, the ceiling with chunks of plaster missing, the faucet that would not stop dripping no matter how many washers you put in it. Everything was running amok: his marriage, his separation—especially his separation—his job. This house.

This house. He should have known when he first saw it that it would be more trouble than it was worth, even though it sounded like a good deal at the time. Located two miles north of the village, on Drake Road toward Kendall, it was a Victorian stick style wooden frame house with bay windows on the north and south ends. The weathered wood siding looked as if it had never been painted, but was in surprisingly good condition for all that. The floorboards on the verandah were loose and some were rotting. The nearest neighbor was a half mile down the road south of him.

The owner was willing to rent it for $300 a month, with an option to buy, as long as Ben was willing to make improvements, and as long as he was not a college student. The house had been on the market for several years.

There were rumors.

One of the rumors was that the place was haunted.

"Last fella lived there," the real estate agent said, "claims he seen blood coming from the walls. College professor."

Ben knew the man, a philosophy instructor and something of a dipso named Spicer who had also claimed to have seen UFOs, conversed with dead relatives on a regular basis, and who had been let go from the college after offering to perform an unnatural act on the president's wife at a party one night. Hardly a reliable source.

Another rumor was that the last family who lived there had died under mysterious circumstances, though the agent insisted there was nothing mysterious about it.

"Carbon monoxide from an old coal furnace. Damn thing was leaking. But I took care of it. Put in an oil furnace."

Ben didn't care why the place was so cheap. Under the circumstances, there hadn't been much choice but to take it. Since he had been let go from the college ("due to financial exigencies," the letter had said), and since Adrienne had asked him to give her "some space," he couldn't afford much else. Even the cheapest efficiency apartments were running $500 a month, hardly affordable on what the bookstore paid him. And he thought it might be fun to spend some time working with his hands instead of being scholarly.

But it hadn't been fun at all. It had been backbreaking work made that much more frustrating by the constantly hooting owl.

Ah, the owl.

He changed into clean clothes and drove in to Hunter's Hideaway.

Hunter's Hideaway was located on Main Street on the north bank of the canal in a building that had originally been an A&P, then a disco. Now, it was designed to look like an authentic log cabin with a picture window. A sign in the window read, "Lottery tickets sold here."

Inside, the store smelled of canvas and linseed oil. Fishing rods lined the wall to his left as he walked in. A six-person tent was set up in the center of the floor, and around it were placed a portable cook stove, a cot, a sleeping bag, a mess kit, and a potted fig tree whose leaves were falling off. The idea was to emulate a wilderness campsite. Above the mock campsite, assorted backpacks and bedrolls dangled from the ceiling like corpses. At the rear of the store stood several display cases filled with guns of all sorts.

A thin woman in her fifties, her red hair peppered with grey, sat on a high stool behind the counter reading *Field and Stream* and drinking diet Mountain Dew. She wore jeans and a faded green sweatshirt with the sleeves cut off at the elbows. The legend on the sweatshirt read, "If you think sex is a pain in the ass, you're doing it wrong."

"Something I can help you with, bud?" Smile lines crinkled around her eyes.

"I'd like to buy a shotgun."

The woman led Ben to the rear of the store and stopped at a display case.

"Got some secondhand ones here do you just fine, save you some money." She took a key ring from her pocket, unlocked a case, and removed a gun from the rack inside. "Here's a nice one. Twelve gauge, single barrel. Cheap. Forty-fie dollars." She handed Ben the gun.

It was heavier than Ben expected it to be, the stock smooth, nearly black, with only a few nicks in it. The barrel, too, had a few nicks and looked more like the heating pipes in his basement than anything else. He held it up to his cheek and sighted down the barrel.

"Y'ever fired one of them things before?" she said.

"Just an M-14 when I was in the army."

"Better brace y'self. She's got a kick like a Denver mule."

Ben resisted asking what a Denver mule kicked like and said he'd take the shotgun and two boxes of buckshot. He handed the woman his credit card. She handed him two forms.

"You got to fill these out. One's for the state, other's for the county."

Then she studied the card for a moment and smiled at him.

"Seen any ghosts yet?" she asked.

"What?"

"You're the fella's got the Farnsworth place."

"How'd you know that?"

"Oh," she said, and winked at him. "A little bird told me."

She fit the credit card into the machine and fixed the charge form over it.

"Well?" she said, drawing the roller across the machine.

"Well what?"

"Seen anything?"

"No," said Ben. "Afraid not."

"Guess a sophisticated fella like you don't believe in that sort of thing, huh?" said the woman, handing Ben the charge form for his signature.

"Guess not," Ben replied.

"You ever hear the story about the Captain?"

"The Captain?"

"Old Captain Farnsworth."

"Can't say that I have." The minute he said it he regretted it. Now the woman would feel free to tell him every ridiculous legend that had grown up around the place since the day it was built.

She leaned forward across the counter on her elbows, glanced to the left, then to the right, as if to make sure there were no spies to overhear their conversation.

"Seems old Captain Farnsworth," she began, "he wasn't a captain, really. Just ran a barge on the Erie Canal in the old days. Anyhow, the story goes the Captain had a wife. Pretty girl, they say she was. There's a picture of her somewhere in the town library somewhere. Her name was Bess. Bess Cutler. She was one of the Cutlers from out by Clarendon. They owned a sawmill out there or something. Burned down so long ago nobody knows where it was. There was supposed to be a town named after them somewhere around here, too, but nobody knows where that was, either."

Ben drummed his fingers against the glass top of the counter in annoyance. Why didn't she get to the point?

"But that doesn't matter. Point is, Bess was supposed to be so pretty that the Captain thought everything that wore pants for twenty miles around was after her. And he made himself so crazy he believed she was messing around with someone whenever he wasn't there.

"The story goes that once when she thought he was gone, he came back to find her messing around with some guy—nobody remembers his name. Anyhow, the Captain walked in on Bess and her boyfriend, in a drunken rage, and took an axe or something to her. Cut her head off. There was blood all over the place. Floors. Walls. Couldn't get rid of it. They found her body in the little sewing room next to the master bedroom. Never did find her head. Some say the Captain buried it in the cellar. Some say he burned it in the stove. No one knows. Point is, the Captain went crazy when he sobered up and found out what he'd done. Went through the whole house trying to cut himself with the axe he killed Bess with. Finally battered his head against the newel post at the bottom of the stairs."

The woman paused dramatically. Ben's stomach turned queasy at the thought of the Captain battering his brains in against a newel post, and felt as if he had walked inadvertently into a very bad horror story.

The woman went on, her voice a whisper.

"Since then, they say the ghost of Bess Farnsworth walks the halls looking for her head. Some say it's the captain looking for the head of her lover. Or looking for forgiveness, depending on which version you believe."

The woman paused, searched Ben's eyes to see if there were any belief in them.

"Interesting story," said Ben.

"You know the fella lived there before you? This fella Spicer?"

"Not personally."

"Strange fella. He bought a shotgun, too." She arched one eyebrow at Ben. "What I hear, he used to bring women in all times of the night. Do awful things to them. Drape everything in black. Dress the women in black leather. Then he'd chain them up in the cellar and get out his whips and do unspeakable things. I hear there'd be awful screams coming from that place all hours of the night. Some of those women'd never be seen again."

Ben decided that this woman was a raving lunatic, and he wanted to get away from her as fast as he could. He put the credit card receipt in his pocket.

"I hear," the woman said—her grin had turned into a leer—"that Spicer used to see blood dripping from the walls of that house. You ever seen anything like that?"

"No," said Ben. "I never did."

Ben handed the woman the forms she had asked him to fill out, picked up the shotgun, and headed toward the door. The woman put the forms into a drawer and closed it.

"Ryan," she called out to him as he turned the handle on the front door. He looked back at her. At that moment she looked to him like a troll.

"Shotgun didn't do Spicer any good," she said.

Ben stored the shotgun in the pantry off the kitchen, the shells on the shelf high up.

He didn't believe in headless ghosts, lurkers in the darkness, mysterious forces, whatever you called them. There were enough real horrors in the real world without resorting to the supernatural. Nevertheless, the red-headed woman's story had unsettled him more than he was willing to admit even to himself, and he decided to check out the sewing room next to his bedroom just for—he told himself—the heck of it. He avoided touching the newel post as he headed up the stairs; there were a few indentations, just large enough to have been made by... He laughed. It was, after all, only a story.

There were stains on most of the walls upstairs, brown stains, water stains, he imagined, though they could have been blood stains.

The sewing room was the quietest room in the house. The tension drained out of him as he stood in the center and looked around. Why didn't he come in here more often? It really was a pleasant little place. He sat in the walnut rocker, the only piece of furniture in the room—it was old enough to have belonged to Bess Farnsworth—and leaned back. Though it was old and it creaked, almost screeched (he could fix that), it was very comfortable. He could have gone to sleep in it. There were brown stains all over the walls in here, too, the largest near the floor on the outside wall. It was about the size of a...woman's head (why had he thought of that?).

"Damn that woman," he said.

He went downstairs and spent the rest of the afternoon ripping up the floorboards of the verandah and putting down new ones. He was half finished when he quit at five o'clock, dragged himself into the kitchen, and drank a half bottle of ale. Then he shuffled into the parlor and collapsed on the sofa. He drank the rest of the ale and closed his eyes for a minute.

A spring from the sofa pushed into his ribs. He turned onto his side. The clock in the hall tick-tocked. He'd have to do something about that. Take off the weights or something. Should have thought of that before.

"Whoo!"

He opened his eyes, sat up. Before him floated a silver rectangle, which, as his eyes came into focus, he recognized as the parlor window. His head ached and his stomach churned. He needed something to eat.

He flicked on the floor lamp and looked at his watch. 11:10.

"Oh, hell," he whispered.

He staggered into the kitchen and punched Adrienne's number on the phone.

Upstairs, a floorboard creaked. A mouse scratched inside the walls.

He let the phone ring nine, ten, eleven times.

"Adrienne?"

There was a silence at the other end of the line.

"What do you want?"

"Listen, Ade, I'm really sorry. I didn't mean for this to happen. I worked on the porch all afternoon. Fell asleep on the couch. And, well..."

He waited for her to say something, anything, but there was nothing, not even the sound of her breathing at the other end of the line.

"Goddamn it, Ade, talk to me."

Still nothing.

"Christ, you act as if I planned this. So I made a mistake. Okay. Tell Kevin I'll make it up to him. Tomorrow I'll...Ade? Adrienne?"

Ben stood holding the phone and staring down at the naked toe that poked up through the hole in his sock. The toe looked as if it were some kind of fungus growing at the end of his sock, as if it had nothing to do with him. He put the phone back into the holder.

He walked into the parlor, turned off the lamp, and sat in the middle of the sofa. He thought about Adrienne. He thought about Kevin. He thought about the bookstore, and about his office—former office—at the college, the books and papers and debris flowing across his desk and onto the floor. He thought about this house. Everything was colliding, jostling together for his attention.

The wind had picked up. Leaves rustled. They sounded like coins jangling together. But there was another sound, something he wasn't quite sure of. He waited, listened. Nothing but the clock. He listened some more.

Something shuffled across the floor above his head.

He started toward the stairs.

"Whoo!"

He went to the kitchen and grabbed the shotgun from the pantry, loaded it, and went outside in his stocking feet. He stood beneath the maple tree and waited. In a few minutes the owl hooted again. He positioned himself so he could get a good shot at it, his back toward the house to make sure he didn't shoot out the bedroom window, the barrel pointed in the direction he had heard the owl, and waited.

"Whooo!"

He squeezed the trigger.

There was an explosion; the gun slammed into his shoulder ("like a Denver mule," he thought), but he had remembered to brace himself and stood firm. In an instant he was showered with maple leaves and feathers. He searched the branches above his head where the owl had been. Nothing. There was nothing but leaves on the ground, either. He must have pulverized the bird.

He circled the tree, kicking at the tufts of grass that needed mowing. Still nothing. He checked the tree once again, and satisfied that his plan had worked, went back to the house.

As he turned the corner, he was blinded by a flash of light. He put a hand up to shield his eyes, and a voice barked, "Drop it right there."

"Who the hell are you?" he called at the light.

"Just put the gun down, pal, slowly. Hands up."

Ben leaned the shotgun against the doorjamb and put his hands over his head. A hatless shadow holding a pistol at arm's length and pointed straight at Ben's head stepped in front of the light. It was then that Ben noticed the blue bubbles flashing on top of the police car parked in his driveway.

"Turn around," said the shadow. "Lean your hands against the wall and spread your legs."

"What's this all about?"

"Shut up."

A rough hand grabbed him by the shoulder and shoved. Ben leaned against the wall and spread his legs.

A pair of rough hands patted him down—"frisked," he supposed the term was—for concealed weapons. The wallet was removed from his back pocket.

"You Benjamin L. Ryan?" the shadow-voice asked.

"Yes, I am." He tried, unsuccessfully, to keep the tremor out of his voice.

"You can turn around now."

Ben turned to find himself facing a man slightly shorter than he was with a torso like a beer keg. Except for a few wisps of black hair directly in the center of his head, he was bald and had a black walrus mustache. His partner, standing slightly behind him and to the right, was taller, skinny, and carried a shotgun.

The man with the walrus mustache handed the driver's license back to Ben.

"I'm officer Conley, this here's officer Craven." Conley jerked his thumb vaguely at Craven without looking at him.

"You live here, Mr. Ryan?"

"I do."

"You just fire this here shotgun?"

"Yes."

Conley shook his head as if he were admonishing a recalcitrant child.

"I don't have anything against gun owners, Mr. Ryan. Fact is, I'm a gun owner myself. But did you know there's a local ord'nance against discharging a weapon in a residential area?"

"Residential?" Ben protested. "The nearest house is a half mile away. There's nothing else but trees and fields between here and the lake."

"It's zoned residential, Mr. Ryan, and you have broke the law. I'm supposed to write you up, issue you a summons, impound your weapon. But I'll tell you what." Conley's teeth, below the black mustache, were white and straight, and his lips curled into what almost looked like a leer. "I'm a nice guy, and you look like a pretty reasonable man to me. So I'm going to let you off with a warning. Don't fire that gun no more. You do, and I'm going to have to come back here and do something about it. You follow me?"

Ben glared at the man, prepared to argue about his constitutional rights, but decided that Conley was probably much stronger than he was and would probably take him in for disturbing the peace, assault, and resisting arrest if he so much as opened his mouth. He clenched his fists and glared at Conley.

"I follow you."

Conley smiled and nodded. "I thought you would." He touched the first two fingers of his right hand to the imaginary brim of an imaginary hat.

"G'night, Mr. Ryan. We'll be watching out for you."

The car backed slowly out of the driveway, then headed south toward the village.

Ben stood stiff-legged on the porch and watched the tail lights disappear. His mind seethed with fantasies of violence. He imagined himself alone in the house, the shotgun his only companion, surrounded by police cars, assault helicopters whirly-birding overhead, and S.W.A.T. teams armed with submachine guns, grenade launchers.

He stormed into the kitchen, put the shotgun back in the pantry, and leaned over the sink, staring at the open drain. A centipede zipped out of the drain and across the porcelain. He squashed it with a water glass.

Through the night he drifted in and out of sleep. When morning came, he was exhausted and his back was killing him. He decided that before the day was out, he would talk to Adrienne face to face, get everything out in the open, and apologize to Kevin, especially to Kevin. He called the bookstore to let them know he wasn't coming in today, but would work a double shift tomorrow. Then he hopped into the car and drove to Adrienne's.

Adrienne's house (funny he should think of it that way) was located in what he (and everyone else in town) thought of as the faculty ghetto. They—he, Adrienne, and Kevin—had lived in one of the older houses (if twenty years can be considered old), one that had been built to look like an ordinary house instead of the fake Georgian mansions and Tudor houses they were now building.

Wally Shaw, the next door neighbor, was mowing grass as Ben pulled into the driveway. Wally looked like a middle-aged, overweight Howdy Doody. Ben hadn't even come to a stop before Wally turned off the lawn mower and sauntered toward Ben, his hands in the pockets of his Bermuda shorts.

"Nice to see you, Ben."

"Hi, Wally."

"They're not here."

Ben glared at Wally as if Wally had just announced he was holding Adrienne and Kevin hostage. Wally grinned back as if proud he had gotten the message right.

"Where are they?"

"Adrienne said she was going to her mother's for a few days, maybe even a week. Kevin went with her."

Damn. Her mother's was in Bangor, Maine. She'd be gone at least a week, maybe two. He was damned if he would chase her across New York state and through New England to catch up with her. It would be late tonight before they got there, if they traveled straight through, although with Adrienne's aversion to driving, they would probably stop somewhere for the night, maybe someplace in New Hampshire. It would be tomorrow night before he could call, and even then he wasn't sure his mother-in-law would let him talk to either one of them.

"Seen any ghosts yet?" Wally giggled.

"What are you talking about?" For a moment, Ben could have sworn that Wally looked like the woman from Hunter's Hideaway.

"Ghosts," said Wally. "There's supposed to be ghosts at the place you're living now."

Ben resisted the urge to punch Wally in the face.

"Ghosts, huh? Well, I'll tell you what, Wally. There *are* ghosts at my place. Hundreds of them. Thousands of them. They ooze out of the walls at night, and they're all hungry for blood, Wally. Human blood. And they've sent me out, Wally, me, to bring them the heart of a jackass."

Ben rolled his eyes, curled his lips in a maniacal sneer, and lurched toward Wally, making claws of his hands. Wally fell back two steps, hands flying from his pockets. He looked as if he were about to cry.

"Well…screw you, Ben. I was just trying to be friendly." He went back to the lawn mower and yanked on the starting cord.

"Friendly, my ass," muttered Ben. The only reason Wally had ever been friendly was so he could look at Adrienne's chest.

Wally was still yanking on the starting cord when Ben backed down the driveway and headed home.

He didn't feel like doing much of anything. The verandah could wait until tomorrow. He opened a bottle of ale, took a sip, and decided to set out more D-Con. Then he wandered from room to room, inspecting everything else that needed to be done.

He took two more bottles of ale from the refrigerator and carried them upstairs. He sat in the old walnut rocker in the sewing room, rubbed his palms over the armrests, smooth with age, drank the ale, and tried to think of absolutely nothing

Ben closed his eyes and rocked. He drifted, slowly, slowly. Something touched his hand.

He opened his eyes, expecting to see a fly, or a moth, or a spider, but there was nothing. The afternoon was still bright and blue, though it was wearing on. He liked this room, wondered why he hadn't decided to sleep in here, then realized it was too small to hold his bed comfortably. And that blood stain in the corner. Not blood, water.

He wondered where Adrienne and Kevin were now.

It occurred to him that they might not be coming back from Maine, that Adrienne had made a decision and the trip to Maine was the first step in that decision. What had happened between them? He knew he still loved her, cared for her, but he also knew that loving was hard work, backbreaking work, and he was simply running out of energy. Maybe that was it. Maybe the two of them had simply run out of energy. Maybe it had nothing at all to do with love, but with energy.

He drank another bottle of ale, napped, fixed himself a supper of canned hash, raw onions, and fried eggs, watched the six o'clock news, read the newspaper, tried not to think of his wife and son. As the sun went down, he felt guilty about not doing anything and decided to finish the verandah. By the time he nailed in the last floorboard, it was dark.

He went into the parlor, lay back on the sofa, and closed his eyes. Adrienne's face swam toward him, her black hair a dark halo, her face thin, severe, reprimanding. Then Kevin's, freckled, pouting, and lost. There were other faces, some he didn't recognize, others he did: the agent's, narrow and pale, streaked with coal dust; Spicer's, long and tubular, hair standing up wild like a prophet's; the woman from Hunter's Hideaway, whose smile curved up like the blade of an axe. In the midst of them all, Bess Farnsworth strode regally, her head tucked in the crook of her arm, grey hair pulled back in a bun, rimless bifocals perched owl-like on the tip of her nose.

Ben's eyes snapped open. He heard a noise. The walnut rocker in the sewing room was rocking back and forth. Slowly, cautiously,

Ben got up from the sofa, passed through the dining room and, as quietly as he could, mounted the stairs. When he reached the landing at the top, he stopped. The air on the second floor was arctic. He shivered, hugged himself with the cold, felt the hair on his arms bristle. The rhythm of the rocking chair filled the house like a heartbeat.

Ben giggled. He must have had too much to drink. That was it. And he was still half asleep. His mind told him everything was all right, there was nothing to be afraid of, but his body wanted to run.

He shuffled down the hall to the sewing room, and when he reached the door, he stopped to listen. The door was closed. He was sure he had left it open. The rocker was still rocking. He turned the doorknob gently and pushed the door open. The rocking stopped. He reached for the light switch, then remembered he hadn't put in a light bulb. His hand dropped to his side. The room was silent now, except for a vague scratching in the wall and the ticking of the clock downstairs. The walnut rocker was still.

The room didn't seem as peaceful as it had this afternoon. In fact, it seemed incredibly empty, as if everything had been drained from it. Darkness surrounded him, sucked at his chest, and he had an overwhelming urge to weep.

"Whoo!" came the sound from across the hall, and again, "Whooo!"

Ben rushed across the hall to his bedroom and leaned out the open window. Directly in front of him, on a branch not ten feet away, stood the blackened outline of the owl. The moonlight sparkled in its eyes.

It wasn't possible!

Ben hurried downstairs to fetch the shotgun and a flashlight, stuffed his pockets with shells, and charged back upstairs.

He loaded the shotgun, placed the flashlight on the window sill and adjusted it until it shone on the owl. The owl didn't move. It merely stared back at him and looked indignant. Ben took careful aim and fired. There was a flutter of wings, a rustling of leaves. Somehow he had missed. The owl now stared at him from a branch three feet higher up and slightly to the right. He readjusted the flashlight, jammed another shell into the breech, aimed again until he saw the owl's eyes at the end of the barrel. He fired.

Again he missed. This time the owl sat below him and to the left. How was it possible? He couldn't have missed this close.

He shoved another shell into the chamber and fired a third time. This time when he looked, there was a hole where the owl had been. He swung the flashlight back and forth, but there was nothing to be seen, nothing to be heard.

He stood for several minutes and listened, just to be sure. The only sound was the rasping of his own breath, the thumping of his own heart.

Then there was another noise. A pounding that at first was barely audible, but which grew until it shook the whole house. It came from downstairs.

He took off his shoes and went down the stairs, one at a time, in his stocking feet.

"Boom…boom…boom," the pounding went on. It seemed to be everywhere, but when he reached the bottom of the stairs he realized it was coming from the kitchen. He flattened himself against the wall and peered around the doorway into the kitchen. Through the glass of the door leading outside, he beheld a dark shadow, something wide and horrible, something that was trying to get in. It had the hugest head he had ever seen, and the head kept moving from side to side as if it were very hungry.

Ben checked to make sure there was a shell in the chamber, and raised the gun to his shoulder. The handle of the kitchen door began to turn. Ben held his breath and tightened his grip on the trigger.

"Ryan, you in there?"

The door swung open, and Officer Conley stepped into the kitchen and stopped.

"Evening, Mr. Ryan. You going to shoot me?"

"Huh? Oh, no." Ben let the gun drop to his side. "You just scared the hell out of me, that's all."

Conley beckoned to him. "Come out here a second," he said. "I want to show you something."

Ben followed Conley out to the yard, shotgun still in his hand, barrel pointed at the ground. Craven appeared from the shadows of the porch and fell in behind Ben.

Conley took Ben to the end of the driveway and stopped at one of the boulders that flanked the drive, turned toward Ben and seized the shotgun.

"Hey, what the..." Ben started, but Conley nodded toward Craven. Ben looked back to see Craven holding his own shotgun waist high and angled up slightly so that if he fired, it would hit Ben squarely in the chest.

"You can't get away with this," said Ben.

Conley ignored him, raised the gun above his head as if it were a sledgehammer, and brought it down against the rock with all his strength. The stock splintered. Conley raised the gun a second time, again smashed it against the rock. This time the stock flew up in the air and landed in the middle of the driveway. Twice more Conley smashed what was left of the gun against the rock to make sure the firing mechanism wouldn't work, and when he was finished, tossed the mangled bit of metal into a ditch.

Conley brushed his hands together, tipped his hat. "There you go, Mr. Ryan. Man who doesn't own a gun can't break the law."

Ben stood speechless as the police car disappeared into the night. He wanted to be enraged, tried to work up his rage, but felt as if all rage, indeed, all emotion had been drained from him.

He shuffled back to the house, up the stairs, his pale, white toe protruding, once again, slug-like from the hole in his sock, to the sewing room. He lowered himself into the walnut rocker and yearned for the serenity of the afternoon, but was aware only of the trembling of his own hands. He felt as if he had been set adrift on an iceflow and was being drawn inexorably toward... what?...and there was nothing he could do about it. Adrienne and Kevin were gone, swallowed up by the wilds of Maine.

Outside the window, the owl hooted. Ben was not surprised. Not at all. He would never be rid of it. It came with the place. He sat in darkness, waiting for the walls to bleed.

He Wasn't There Again Today

Half way up the stairs, Jessica Martin stopped. Nothing was on the landing. Something like a cold hand slid up her back. It started at the cleft above her buttocks and worked its way toward the base of her skull.

She gripped the railing with her right hand and tried very hard to focus her eyes. Nothing was still on the landing. It did not look like a little man about three feet tall with no eyes that did not lick out at her like flames and a black bowler not perched squarely on the center of his head. The little man did not have a long beard all knotted and matted, and when he did not smile, she saw no teeth pointed and sharp like fangs and not ready to bite her.

The baby babbled from the kitchen behind her.

She closed her eyes and prayed quickly that he would go away, but when she opened them, he was still not there. Slowly she backed down the stairs, fearful he would not come after her, and retreated to the kitchen. She leaned over the sink, eyes closed, heart pounding so loudly it seemed to echo.

In her head rang the words of the poem her mother had once recited to her, the poem that had started the whole thing:

> *Last night I spied upon the stair*
> *A little man who wasn't there*
> *He wasn't there again today*
> *Oh, how I wish he'd go away.*

It had seemed a silly poem at the time, as most things do when you are four, and she and her mother laughed and laughed at the idea of being able to see something that was not there. But it stopped being funny the night her mother said to stay in bed while her parents went out, and just to make sure, mother was going to ask the little man to stand outside Jessica's door.

And that was the first time Jessica had seen the little man not standing right outside her bedroom door, waiting for her to disobey her mother. Then, oh boy, would she be sorry, and he grinned that nasty little not grin at her and exposed those nasty little not teeth for the first time, saliva dripping from them like venom.

Her mother had used the little man for years to make sure that Jessica behaved.

"If you don't behave," Beatrice Peckham had warned in that singsong voice she had, and that half smile that let you know this might be a joke, but you could never be sure, "I'll have to call the little man."

Then she had laughed and laughed in that way she had to let Jessica know this was all in fun, except that to Jessica it wasn't funny, especially in the middle of the night when she had to get up to go to the bathroom and found the little man not standing outside her bedroom door, and she stood, paralyzed with terror, unable to move, until finally she couldn't hold it any longer and wet her nighty.

Her mother would become very angry, pushing the urine-soaked nighty up to Jessica's nose and yelling at her that she was getting too old to wet herself and there must be something dreadfully wrong with her.

"But mama," Jessica had cried. "The little man wouldn't let me."

"There is no little man. It's just a stupid little poem. Honestly, Jessica. I don't see where you get these lies from."

"But he's real. He really is. I saw him."

And her mother had slapped her across the mouth.

"Don't you lie to me, young lady. You were just too lazy to get out of bed. You're worse than your father."

Even now as she stood in the kitchen and watched Rebecca chewing on the corner of a rubber alphabet block, she could hear her mother's voice admonishing her.

"It's all in your mind, Jessica. You always have had an overactive imagination."

Which was another one of her mother's ways of telling her she was crazy, that nothing she remembered, or thought she remembered, from her childhood was true. But Jessica knew she wasn't crazy, knew certain things had happened, were still vivid in her mind, were not even repressed memories, as psychologists had sometimes called them.

She had never forgotten, for example, the time a little boy from down the street—she couldn't remember his name, if she had ever known it—had brought her flowers, violets and dandelions, and stood at the front door, grinning and blushing. She wanted to accept the flowers, but her mother said she couldn't go out and no one could come in. And she couldn't open the door, either. You never knew what kind of people were wandering around the neighborhood these days. But Jessica had figured out a way to get around her mother's warning. She went to one of the drawers in the kitchen and took a steak knife and cut a hole in the bottom corner of the screen door, and the boy handed the flowers to her through the hole, just about the time her mother was walking into the kitchen.

Her mother yelled at the boy and told him never to come near this house again—and he hadn't. Jessica never saw him again. Then Beatrice Peckham tossed the flowers into the waste basket and dragged Jessica by one arm down into the basement and told her she had to stay there for three days, until she learned enough not to cut holes in screen doors. For those three days, Jessica lived on oatmeal and orange juice, served to her twice a day, at breakfast and dinner time. Her mother set up a little cot with blankets over in one corner, and told her she had to sleep without her dolls or her teddy bear. And worst of all, though her mother never summoned him, the little man appeared, not guarding the stairs to make sure she didn't try to sneak up when her mother wasn't looking.

Jessica trembled at the memory, glad her mother was dead, and picked up Rebecca from the playpen just to hold her, to feel the certainty of her being, to make sure she was all right.

"Is something wrong?" said Tom Martin, when he came home from work. Jessica didn't tell him what had happened. He knew what Beatrice Peckham had been like, knew almost everything that had happened to Jessica growing up, including the episode in the basement, but Jessica had never told him about the little man and couldn't do it even now. He might think she was crazy.

"Are you sure you're okay, Jessie? You look a little pale."

"I'm okay. Just had a little flashback today."

"Mother?"

"Mother."

"Do you need to talk about it?"

Jessica felt lucky that Tom had come into her life. He was always willing to listen to her without making judgments. But she couldn't do it just now.

"Not right now. It's sweet of you to offer. Maybe in a couple of days."

"When do you see Margaret again?"

"Wednesday. I'll talk to her then and see what she says. I don't mean to keep you out of this, Tom. But I need to talk to Margaret first, and then I promise we'll talk."

"Okay. I just get worried about you."

"Do you think I'm crazy?" Jessica asked.

Margaret Estridge crossed her legs and recrossed them, left over right. She adjusted the hem of her skirt, brushing away an imaginary particle of lint, and looked straight at Jessica.

"Do you think you're crazy?"

Jessica sat with her legs tucked up underneath her. She could get away with that today because she was wearing a pair of old jeans and a white Big Bird sweatshirt. She wouldn't have done that if she'd been wearing a skirt, even if it was only Margaret in the room. That's just the way she had been brought up, the way her mother had taught her. Her sneakers lay on the floor, one leaning sideways against the other. She thought about Margaret's question for a moment.

"No," she said. "I don't think so. But I asked you and you threw it back to me. That's not fair."

Margaret reached over and rested her hand on Jessica's knee for a moment, then withdrew it. "You're not crazy. But I do think you are getting close to some core issues and that is why the little man has reappeared."

"Then you believe he's real?"

"I believe you believe he's real."

Jessica leaned back in her chair. That was the best she was going to get from Margaret, the best she could expect. Even Jessica herself found it hard to believe in the little man's existence. After all, she really had not seen him.

"I know what you mean, Margaret, but this whole thing is difficult to explain."

"Do you need to explain it?"

"Yes, of course. I don't want *you* to think I'm crazy."

The women laughed.

"What is it you need to explain?"

Jessica closed her eyes for a minute and took a deep breath. She tried to get a clear image in her mind of what she wanted to say, what words she could choose to express what it was she needed to express. She wanted to get a clear image of him. But the images swam around in her mind like goldfish in a bowl, refused to settle in any one place long enough for her to get a good look at them. All she could imagine were things associated with him: the black bowler hat the size of a stew pot, the black beard all knotted and kinky that came to a slightly rounded V.

"Jessica, I want you to think about the first time you saw him. Can you do that?"

"Well, I've never exactly seen him. It's more like I've seen him not being there."

"I don't follow you."

"I don't mean that he's not there. I mean he's NOT there. He's there and not there. It's as if absence has become tangible, palpable, audible. I can even hear him not breathing."

Margaret again looked straight at Jessica and nodded, not so much in agreement or understanding as in acceptance that what Jessica was saying was what Jessica understood.

"Regardless. I believe you said that the first time was when your mother left you alone."

"Y-yes."

"And when was the last time you saw that he was...not there?"

"I don't remember exactly. I think I was a teenager."

"And what happened when you were a teenager?"

"Nothing especially. I got older, had friends. Stopped believing in ghosts and goblins."

"And what about your mother? Was she still abusing you?"

"No. She stopped."

"Stopped?"

Jessica hated it when Margaret did that, repeated what she had just said so she would go on. It was one of those techniques that therapists and counselors used to get you to keep talking when you wanted to run and hide.

"I was too big to lock in the cellar anymore. I wouldn't go. I wouldn't do what she asked because I was taller than she was, and I knew I could go over to my girlfriend Patty's house. They knew what my mother was like, even though everyone else thought she was a saint. Besides, she was nearly sixty by then, and I don't think she had the energy to do it anymore. And by that time she had just stopped caring about everything.

"The other thing was that my father had stopped traveling so much. She wouldn't dare do that when he was home."

"And the little man?"

"What about the little man?"

"Did he still come?"

"No. What are you saying, Margaret?"

"I'm not saying anything, Jessica. I heard you say that the little man first came when your mother first threatened you with him, and that he stopped coming when she stopped abusing you."

"Then you think he's just some hallucination that my mind conjured up from some childhood trauma? Isn't that just another way of saying I'm crazy, delusional?"

Margaret uncrossed her legs and leaned forward. She reached out and held Jessica's hand in hers, softly stroking it as she spoke, her voice warm and soothing.

"Jessica, listen to me. What you've experienced is not unusual and it's not crazy. It's real. Sometimes we seem to outgrow our childhood traumas, only to have them resurface later in life at some crucial juncture. In your case, this little man was a tool that your mother used to abuse you, to keep you under her control and terrified. Even though she never touched you, the threat was always there, and sometimes the threat is actually worse than a physical blow. When you were old enough that she could no longer control you, her weapon was no longer useful. The little man went away, or seemed to go away. But he never really went away because you were never given the opportunity to confront the abuse. You were told it never happened, that you were making things up, or seeing things.

"And now what's happened to bring him back? Well, you're a young bride…"

"Margaret, I'm thirty-one, for God's sake."

"Thirty-one is not old, Jessica. But if it makes you more comfortable, you are a relatively new bride, a wife, a conscientious teacher, and now you are a new mother. There is a lot of pressure in your life right now. So it makes perfect sense to me that the little man would reappear after all these years."

Jessica's hand began to shake. She could feel the terror whelming up inside her, spreading up her back, across her shoulders, and rushing through her head until the tears started leaking from her eyes.

Margaret knelt beside her and held her. Jessica rocked back and forth in the woman's arms, tears coursing through her as if they were being pumped from some deep and hidden source inside her. She thought she would never stop, would go on and on crying out in fear, in terror, until there was nothing left of her.

But, eventually, the tears began to ebb, and she found her head aching from having cried so much. Margaret held out a box of tissues. Jessica took a handful and blew her nose into them, one after the other. Then she settled back, totally exhausted.

"My God, Margaret. What am I going to do?"

She dabbed at the corner of her eyes with the tissue and blew her nose again.

"You need to confront him."

"What?"

"It's all right, Jessica. We won't do that today. Next time. Would you be willing to do a role play the next time?"

"Jesus, I don't know. What if I see him before that?"

"You'll have to face him, let him know that you can't be intimidated. Swear at him, yell at him if it will help. Or you can call me. The point is, Jessica, that you are the only one who can do anything about him."

"Your eyes are all red. What happened?"

Jessica looked at her husband and felt the tears rising up in her again. She didn't want to cry again, didn't want to cry in front of him, even though she knew it would be all right. He was the only man she had ever met who wasn't frightened by a woman's tears, wasn't intimidated or embarrassed, and who didn't look at them as a sign of weakness. That was one of the reasons she had married him. Another reason was that he hadn't been afraid to let her see him cry. Just a few weeks before they were married, he sat in the living room of her apartment and openly wept, telling her of his fears of being a failure to her as a husband and the father of their children, and his fear of becoming like his own father, who had spent most of his adult life bouncing from one mistress to another and ignoring his own wife and children.

The last time she had seen him cry was the morning Rebecca was born, and she recalled him still, the tears streaming down his cheeks and into his beard as the two of them cuddled the new miracle that had entered their life.

"I saw Margaret today." And then she could hold back no longer. "Oh, Tommy. It was just awful."

Tom enveloped her in his arms, cradling his right hand gently against the back of her head, his left arm supporting her back. She sobbed for several minutes. When it was over, Tom said, "Do you want to tell me now?"

"Of course," she said. "Just give me a few minutes to catch my breath. Why don't you go up and change. I'll make us a drink, and I'll meet you in the living room."

Tom went upstairs. She heard him moving around, then walking into the bathroom. A few moments later the toilet flushed.

Jessica took two glasses from the cupboard and set them on the counter. She took some ice from the freezer and put a couple of ice cubes in each glass. Then she put in a shot of vodka, filled each glass to the top with tonic, and topped each with a wedge of lime. She picked up the glasses and started toward the living room but stopped abruptly. Something was wrong. Rebecca was playing quietly in her playpen. It wasn't Rebecca.

Still, Jessica felt that coldness snaking up her back the way it had a few days ago. Tom was moving about upstairs, and she could tell from his footsteps that he was on his way downstairs. She put the glasses down on the table and started out to the hall when she heard Tom yell, "Oh shit," then something crashed to the bottom of the stairs. By the time she reached the landing, he was already unconscious, his head twisted around at an odd angle, his legs awry, pointing up.

She thought she heard laughter, like dry leaves being crushed, and she turned her head toward the sound. He was not sitting on the very top stoop, arms not folded across his knees, the bearded chin not resting on his folded arms, that nasty grin, wide as a scythe, not slicing across his face.

"God, no," she screamed, swinging back toward Tommy and falling to her knees by his side.

"Tommy, Tommy," she cried. "Are you okay? Can you hear me? Please be okay, Tommy. Godammit, answer me."

She put one hand over her own mouth to keep the panic in and reached for her husband's pulse with the other. She had to make sure he was alive. She placed the first two fingers against his wrist, not too hard, but firmly enough to feel if there was a pulse, and breathed a sigh of relief when she felt it, not quite as strong as she had hoped, but strong enough to know that he wasn't dead, that he might really be okay. Then she ran to the kitchen phone and punched in 911.

By the time she finished explaining what had happened and where she lived and got back to her husband, she could no longer see the little man.

Tommy had broken both legs and his left wrist. He had a couple of cracked vertebrae and a mild concussion and would have to spend a few weeks in the hospital, but otherwise he should be all right.

"He's a very lucky man," the doctor told her, though she failed to see how someone with two broken legs and everything else could be considered lucky.

Jessica waited at the hospital most of the night. Tom's mother, Kathy, was kind enough to take Rebecca home and said Jessica could stay with them, too, if she didn't want to be alone. Jessica said she would see.

When Jessica talked with Tom the following day, he couldn't remember a thing.

"One minute I'm walking out of the bedroom, the next minute I'm here looking up at the ceiling with the worst damn headache I've ever had in my life."

He smiled up at her, and she tried to smile back at him and squeezed his right hand, the only thing that didn't have a cast on it.

"Funny thing, though," he continued. "I had this really weird dream, but I can only remember one thing about it."

"What's that?"

"Just this damn midget in a black derby hat."

Jessica stayed with Tom's mother for a couple of days until she started to feel a little less anxious about Tom. Kathy didn't mind, though. She was delighted to have Rebecca with her, even though she, too, was worried about Tom. But three days were enough, and over Kathy's protests that she deserved to be pampered a little, Jessica took Rebecca home.

The house was quiet, peaceful. Jessica took a tour of the house, starting with the basement and even checking the closets, just to make sure. She held Rebecca the whole time, even though Rebecca did her best to squirm out of her mother's arms, grasping hold of her hair several times and yanking. Once she had assured herself that everything was safe, she placed Rebecca in the kitchen playpen and fixed dinner for the two of them.

Several times during the last few days, she had wanted to ask Tom more about his dream, to see if she could elicit more details from him. Maybe it was just a dream, just a coincidence, but she was sure that Tommy, too, had seen the little man. And if Tommy had seen him, then she wasn't crazy. That would be proof. She didn't want to upset him when he was in such physical pain. She decided to wait until he was better.

She called Margaret to let her know what had happened and how worried she was about her husband, but she didn't say anything about the little man. She was sure that if she told Margaret that the little man had pushed Tom, or tripped him—or was it that he had not pushed Tom, not tripped him?—Margaret would be sure Jessica was delusional, no matter what she actually said.

It occurred to her that what had happened to Tommy was a warning, a message from the little man that he could do whatever he wanted, get away with whatever he could, and she was powerless to stop him. She didn't want to believe that. She wanted to believe Margaret, that the little man was a weapon her mother had used, and she needed to confront him in order to be free.

When dinner was ready, Jessica strapped the baby into the high chair so she couldn't slide out and put the little sectioned dish in front of her. Rebecca hadn't quite figured out how to get everything in her mouth yet, so some of the creamed spinach ended up in her hair, some mashed on her bib, and some on the floor. Jessica laughed at her daughter, and Rebecca giggled back. She thought dinner time was such fun.

After she bathed Rebecca and put her to bed, Jessica took a hot shower, put on a nightgown and a robe, and tried to watch a little television. She flicked from channel to channel, but could find nothing to hold her attention. Then she tried reading for a while, though she still couldn't concentrate on what she was reading. She started to feel drowsy.

She was nodding off when she heard Rebecca babbling to herself upstairs. Jessica opened her eyes and smiled. The baby sounded so happy, so content.

It was at that point that Jessica felt a certain uneasiness, nothing very specific, but a vague sense that something was not quite right. She looked around the living room for something to be out of place—the coffee table, the lamp, the television, Tommy's recliner—but everything was normal. There was a slight odor, though, something like dead mice or day-old garbage. She was sure she had taken out the trash. Maybe something was still in the garbage disposal.

She stood up and started toward the kitchen. Rebecca was giggling now, as if someone were in there playing with her, tickling her. The odor grew stronger, more pungent. Now it smelled like sweat, like menstrual blood, rotten eggs. The smell began to overpower her, pushed against her face like a hand trying to hold her back.

Rebecca was laughing now, actually laughing, and Jessica knew, could feel with her entire body that something was terribly, terribly wrong. The chill started in her vagina and spread like acid to her thighs and up her torso until every molecule in her tingled. Rebecca. Something was happening to Rebecca.

Jessica ran to the stairs, and with one hand on the banister, stopped.

It was him.

She could see him.

He was there. And he was holding Jessica, tossing her up in the air and catching her, making her laugh, the way Tommy did. Tommy.

When he saw Jessica standing at the bottom of the stairs, her right hand on the banister, her left foot frozen on the first step, he stared straight at her. Rebecca cooed in his arms, her tiny hand entangled in his beard. The razor grin spread across his face, wider and wider until Jessica thought it would never stop, thought it would consume the room, the whole house and everything in it.

Jessica knew that he had come as if to fulfill some covenant that had been made in childhood, a covenant that had never been spoken, had never even been thought of and for which she had no name, but one that needed to be honored nonetheless.

"Put her down, you son of a bitch," she screamed. "It's me you want."

The little man made no sound, said no words, but turned and put the baby down on the bedroom floor as gently as if she were a carton of eggs, and closed the door. Then he faced Jessica at the top of the stairs.

Neither of them moved, and in that moment Jessica had a good look at him for the very first time, the hydrocephalic head larger than a dinner plate, and the eyes so black and endless they seemed to be without retinas. There was no torso. There was just the head with all its teeth, then the arms with those grasping, filthy hands at the end, and the thick, short legs.

Without any warning, the little man leaped at her from the top of the stairs, and before the thought had even registered, his hands were around her throat. Her head banged against the wall, and she tumbled to the floor, the little man on top of her. His face was right above her, his fetid breath pushing its way into her mouth and up her nostrils, gagging her with the smell of garlic, of animal musk, of decaying sea creatures washed up on the shore. And those teeth, so close, so close they seemed to fill the world.

Terror gripped her, paralyzed her. She could feel her body stiffen, turning to stone. She had to do something, had to stop the paralysis, or she would die, be dead, and the little man would take Rebecca and Tommy and everything in the world that had ever mattered to her and he would win, and mother would win.

The thought of her mother winning sent a jolt through her, and she burst through her paralysis. With her left hand she reached up and grabbed his right ear, sinking her nails as far in as she could go, and with her right hand reached up between his legs to where she imagined his testicles must be and squeezed as hard as she could.

There was no scream, no sound at all, but the little man's grin turned into a grimace, his mouth widened as if he were screaming, and his hands let go of her throat.

She seized the opportunity and flung him away from her. He crashed against the wall, and before he reached the floor, Jessica had rolled herself to her feet.

She wanted to run to the kitchen, get one of those carving knives from the holder beside the refrigerator, but she only managed two steps when the little man came after her again. He tackled her behind the knees and sank his teeth into her thigh. She screamed in pain and crashed to the floor, hitting her head against the stove. Everything blurred, and she felt herself losing consciousness, darkness bleeding toward the edge of her awareness. She couldn't pass out now, couldn't let go now. Everything depended upon her ability to stay awake. She willed herself not to pass out, forced back the darkness, tacked against that soothing lethargy that wooed her to let go, relax, drift, and gradually the darkness dwindled and she was swimming upward.

Her eyes snapped open and she felt him forcing himself up, prying her thighs apart, his jaws snapping their way wildly toward her crotch. She cocked her left leg back and kicked her foot squarely into his face. The little man went flying across the kitchen and smashed against the refrigerator. Knives scattered across the counter.

Jessica pulled herself up and grabbed the first thing within her reach, which happened to be a water kettle. She spun around as the little man charged at her one more time, and she swung as hard as she could, bringing the kettle down as if it were a golf club and catching the little man just under his jaw.

He staggered back. Water went flying everywhere. She swung again, and this time caught him square in the face. Blood gushed from his nose and mouth as he sprawled backwards and rolled. Jessica hesitated a moment and stared. He seemed to be getting smaller, but before she could even think about it, he leaped at her, blood and spittle flying, his teeth bared and biting. She hit him again, but he kept coming back.

Somehow, she managed to maneuver herself over to the refrigerator to where the knives had fallen, and while the little man was recovering from another one of her blows, she grabbed the knife closest to her, a ten-inch cook's knife with a very sharp point.

As he launched himself at her, she swung the knife around and held it out straight in front of her. He saw the knife too late and, in midair, impaled himself up to the hilt. The impact jolted her back a step, but she steadied herself against the refrigerator and started forward. Still he flailed at her, the knife jutting out through his back like a needle through a cockroach. Blood flowed from what she thought must be his chest all over her hands and arms, and she almost slipped as she tried to carry him toward the kitchen sink. But she held him out in front of her, while he struggled wildly in a desperate attempt to free himself.

She stumbled to the sink, and with one hand grabbed him by the neck, and with the other switched on the garbage disposal. His skin was cold and slimy, and she shivered in revulsion, but held on. The little man's eyes grew wide with panic, blood and spittle still bubbled from his mouth, but still there was no sound except the beating of her own heart. She shoved one of his stubby legs down into the opening and he began to shudder and thrash more violently. He turned his head from side to side, snapping his jaws open and shut in an attempt to bite her. But the garbage disposal took hold and pulled him in, a little at a time. She pulled the knife from his chest and blood gushed all over the sink. The garbage disposal ground away. Blood and bone flew everywhere, spattering against her face, her hair, the kitchen window, the curtains, but she held fast. He reached his arms up in an attempt to grab hold of her, but she slapped them away. The garbage disposal sucked him in, slowly, slowly, until there was nothing left showing except his head with its gnashing teeth, now reddened with his own blood, and one raised hand that opened and closed like a baby's fist.

Jessica let go and stared in horror as the machine took in the head, leaving only the baby's fist, and then taking that, too. The baby's fist.

"Oh my God," she cried, as recognition broke over her. "Oh, my God, no. What have I done?"

"Rebecca," she screamed. "Jesus, no. Jesus, no."

All she could see was that little fist, opening and closing in desperation as it vanished down the drain.

She ran from the kitchen, slipping in the blood that coated the floor, and half climbed, half stumbled up the stairs.

She stopped outside Rebecca's door, not wanting to open it, not wanting to know what was really true, and gulped in large breaths of air. Then she swung the door open. She flipped on the light switch and ran over to the crib.

Rebecca was gone, her blankets tossed aside. A keening sob escaped from Jessica's lips, and she sank down in despair. She clutched the baby's blanket close to her face, sobs erupting from deep inside her stomach, from some source of pain she had never known existed before, when she heard a faint cry from the corner. She stopped in mid-sob and held in her breath. Silence filled the room like fog, and then she heard it again. She spun around to see Rebecca sitting there, her diaper very wet, her pajamas soaked through. Jessica scooped her up and hugged her, smearing blood all over the child.

"Oh, Becca. Becca, thank God, Becca. Thank God."

She gave Rebecca another bath, dressed her in a clean diaper and pajamas, then put her back to bed and sang her a song until her eyes closed and she was asleep. Then Jessica went downstairs. There was blood all over the kitchen and hall. Some pieces of pottery were broken, the kitchen table had been overturned, and one chair was smashed

By the time she finished cleaning, it was nearly dawn. She threw her bloodied clothing in the washing machine, lumbered upstairs, and soaked in a hot bath.

She would have to call Margaret and tell her what had happened. Maybe not everything, maybe not all the details. Margaret would be sure she was crazy. But she would tell Margaret she was no longer afraid of the little man; she had defeated him and knew he no longer had the power over her that he once did.

Perhaps she would tell Tommy, too, but not just yet. Tommy wouldn't think she was crazy. He loved her too much.

Jessica dried herself and put on a fresh nightgown. Then she climbed into bed and pulled up the covers. Just before she dozed off, she heard a gentle wind soughing through the trees. It sounded like low laughter, like dry leaves being crushed.